LORD CORSAIR

Beastly Lords Book Seven

A Novella

SYDNEY JANE BAILY

cat whisker press
Massachusetts

First published as A Pirates of Britannia World Novel, 2019.

ISBN: 978-1-957421-39-1
Published by Cat Whisker Press
Editor: Chloe Bearuski
Cover: Philip Ré
Book Design: Cat Whisker Studio

DEDICATION

To Janet (née Baily) Wilson

If there was a medal for kindness, thoughtfulness,
and being a superb aunt,
I would bestow it upon you. I love you!

OTHER WORKS
by
SYDNEY JANE BAILY

The RAKES ON THE RUN Series

Last Dance in London
Pursued in Paris
Banished to Brighton
Gretna Green by Sunset

The RARE CONFECTIONERY Series

The Duchess of Chocolate
The Toffee Heiress
My Lady Marzipan

The DEFIANT HEARTS Series

An Improper Situation
An Irresistible Temptation
An Inescapable Attraction
An Inconceivable Deception
An Intriguing Proposition
An Impassioned Redemption

The BEASTLY LORDS Series

Lord Despair
Lord Anguish
Lord Vile
Lord Darkness
Lord Misery
Lord Wrath
Lord Corsair
Eleanor

PRESENTING LADY GUS

A Georgian-Era Novella

ACKNOWLEDGMENTS

I offer heartfelt gratitude to *my own* Philip, who listens whether I'm discussing plot, characters, details of ship's sails, or the history of pirates, which is the best gift in the world.

And I thank my readers. I love hearing from you. Whenever you tell me you've enjoyed one of my stories, it's like receiving a warm hug.

CHAPTER ONE

1851, Bias Bay, South China Sea

P hilip Carruthers leaped onto the deck of the Chinese pirate ship, letting his men secure the small two-masted junk while he headed for the captain's cabin in the stern. He had one prize to obtain though he had to fight through more pirates than he cared for.

Too many bloody pirates, he thought, as two men rushed him.

Still, with his pepperbox revolver in one hand and a sword in the other, he fancied his odds were good and quickly dispatched both pirates to Davy Jones's locker.

Since the carriage accident that took Robert's life, Philip continued to hear him in his head as the voice of reason.

Besides that, the only thing left of his brother was a—

"Arr," he yelled as he broke the door down to the pirate captain's cabin. The man himself was on deck, as Philip had seen, and was undoubtedly engaged in battle with his crew, if not already tied up or killed.

In the cabin, Philip hoped to find the treasure he had been seeking for two long years.

As he crashed through the doorway, he saw two things at once. Rising from the bed was a woman, her hair in disarray, wearing a decidedly ragged gown and an expression of terror. Secondly, also on the bed, was a small, red-lacquered box, leather straps around it for security. It was as if everything important had been gathered together in one spot by the pirate captain.

How tidy!

Philip stopped in his tracks. He'd been expecting the latter but certainly not the former—a white woman, in Bias Bay, on a Chinese pirate junk.

What the hell? The captain's mistress?

Raising his weapon toward her, he asked, "Who are you?"

"Beryl Angsley," she said evenly, her fear apparently having dissipated somewhat when he hadn't instantly killed her. "Daughter of Lord Harold Angsley."

A peer's daughter. She said it as if introducing herself at a ball.

Christ!

He shook his head and sheathed his sword. This was not his day. First, he'd nearly missed this slinky ship he'd been pursuing for two weeks. In the waning light, the junk almost slipped past him and out to the open waters where they would have lost her for sure. Then some of the pirates, either cowardly or clever, had hidden behind barrels on the junk's deck instead of engaging in honest battle the instant his men boarded.

Thus, Philip had seen one of his crew lose a hand before his eyes from the surprise attack.

Losing a hand over jewels! Dammit!

At least the man hadn't forfeited his life. Philip prided himself on not losing a single member of his crew since setting out from the docks of London two years earlier, neither from desertion nor death. His goal, besides the contents of the glossy container, was to get the crew of the *Robert* home safely to their loved ones, not to go home and give terrible news to widows and orphans. He would consider it a personal failure to lose even one man.

Now, to be saddled with an Englishwoman, here on the other side of the bloody globe in the South China Sea, it had to be a stroke of the worst luck. For Philip couldn't leave her behind.

"You are a prisoner?"

She nodded.

"From now on you are simply, Beryl Angsley, daughter of no one in particular."

She opened her mouth—a pretty one, too—perhaps to protest, but he interrupted her.

"The higher your social status, the greater your ransom value, the more danger you are in. Even among my own crew."

Philip was wasting valuable time. They were in pirate-infested waters and other junks, under the leadership of Chui-A-poo, were undoubtedly sailing toward them even then. And at that moment, his own ship, a swift and small clipper, had a skeleton crew until they secured this vessel and returned to her, meaning vulnerability of the worst sort.

Once back aboard her, however, the *Robert* could outrun practically anything.

He turned his attention to the other item, the treasure for which he'd risked life and limb, the small container still on the bed. It didn't need to be very large to contain what he sought. It looked exactly as had been described to him one dark night in a tavern in Ningbo, just south of Shanghai, a month prior.

Still, he had to be certain. As he walked toward her, the woman darted sideways and around him. Even as he bent to pick up the box, he spied her out of the corner of his eye moving toward the splintered door.

"Don't go out there," he uttered without looking.

She halted.

"It'll mean your death and not a clean one, I can assure you."

Drawing the knife from his boot, in the blink of an eye, he sliced off the leather straps and opened the intricately worked metal clasp. Lifting the lid, he checked inside. From a bed of black satin, a necklace of rubies, diamonds, and gray pearls winked at him in the light of the cabin's lamps. The man in Ningbo hadn't lied.

It had been a long hunt to recover the jewelry belonging to the Duchess of Sutherland, stolen unbelievably from her quarters at Buckingham Palace. When next he returned to Britain, he would receive a generous, well-deserved bounty.

Placing the container in a bag slung over his shoulder, Philip turned to Miss Angsley. He had no choice, he reminded himself. She was an Englishwoman.

"Let's go."

She frowned, and it didn't mar her lovely features one bit, he noted.

"But you said *not* to go out there," she protested.

"Not without me. My men are in full fight mode and on high alert. Let me smooth the way, stay close, and you'll be fine."

"You're the captain?" *Was that doubt in her tone?*

"Yes."

"For the British Navy, I take it, by your accent."

"Alas, no. I run a private ship on commission."

"Private or *pirate*, did you say?"

"Same thing," he muttered, grasping her hand and yanking her behind him as he made his way above deck.

He wished he could tell her to keep her eyes closed because there was more than one unpleasant scene unfolding, but he couldn't. All he could do was get her swiftly back to his ship and safely into his cabin.

At her appearance on deck, he heard and felt the change. First, an outcry from the Chinese pirates, most likely at the loss of their prisoner, followed by a murmuring from his own crew as they saw her, and then a definite lessening of the violence. No one wanted to slice a neck open and have blood shooting everywhere in the presence of a woman if it could be helped.

Or so he thought. The pirate captain, a man who would face the wrath of the fleet leader, Chui-A-poo, struggled against his bindings, shrieking at his men to "save the jewels." These words in Chinese, Philip understood.

So, it wasn't the loss of the lady causing the agitation. It was the pirate captain's guess, and perfectly correct, that Philip had taken the red-lacquered box. A few of the Chinese pirates were still fighting and redoubled their efforts at their captain's cries.

"Move smartly!" Philip commanded his men. "More junks in this bay than rats on a barge."

Chui-A-poo had fifty ships under his command—a desperate pirate leader with a price on his head for brutally killing two English officers. Now losing the priceless necklace belonging to Queen Victoria's special friend, Chui would be a dangerous man indeed.

Moving swiftly, Philip crossed the deck, keeping an eye out for Leo, who nearly always accompanied him when he boarded another ship. Spying the fluffy orange tail of the stout cat racing toward him, he led Miss Angsley past the junk's lowered rectangular sails, which he admired for their superior speed and control. The pirates would have them up again in a flash, but he was confident his clipper could outrun them.

Of course, he could order the deaths of enough of the pirate crew to cripple the vessel, but it wasn't his style.

He was called *Lord Corsair*, not *Blackbeard*, for God's sake.

SAFELY BACK ON THE *Robert*, Philip turned his unwanted guest over to his trusted first mate, Rufus, a fierce, red-headed Scot, and then stayed on deck until all his crew had returned and the ship had set sail.

"All hands, haul the wind," he ordered his crew. "Let's get out of here."

"Boom about!" he heard Bantam, his sail master, call out, and then they were underway.

Leaving the Chinese junk behind in the waning light, Philip didn't relax or stop scanning the waters until two hours and about forty nautical miles separated him from Bias Bay. They headed south toward Hong Kong harbor, with no other sails in sight, and, at their current pace, they would be there before midnight.

With the sack still on his back, Philip left the quarterdeck for his cabin in the stern. At his instructions, Rufus had taken Miss Angsley there, for nowhere else on board the ship was suitable for a lady. Besides, it seemed the safest place for her, hopefully, *short* stay.

A single lamp burning, she lay stretched out on his bed, fully clothed, eyes closed, apparently sleeping with her hands together on her chest like a church effigy.

Hesitating, he wondered what to do.

Closing the door quietly behind him, he supposed he should awaken her, ask her some questions, determine if she had family in China, and then decide the most expedient way to get her off his ship.

Instead, he let her sleep. God's teeth but he was exhausted, too. While she slept, so could he. Quietly, he pushed aside the tin full of lead shot for his revolver and slowly lowered his sack to the table, resting it on the charts already there. Then he sat down in his comfortable chair, lifting his booted feet to the table as well.

Leaning his head back, he closed his eyes, knowing he could nod off in a minute, maybe less.

The lookout would alert him at the first sign of danger. Otherwise, the *Robert* would drop anchor in the British-owned and patrolled waters around Queen Victoria's easily won prize of Hong Kong Island.

Beryl awakened with an immediate sense of panic from a fitful sleep filled with nightmarish dreams. She knew at once she was on a ship by the distinct smell of a closed cabin, by the sound of water lapping against the hull, and by the gentle swaying motion, of course.

However, she was no longer aboard the junk, with everyone speaking so quickly in a language she hadn't been able to make neither heads nor tails of since arriving in the Orient two months earlier.

Truly, being unable to communicate, even to ask to relieve herself had been the most terrifying part of her previous ordeal with the Chinese pirates.

Precisely where she was now, she couldn't say, though she hoped still in the South China Sea. All she knew for certain was her father would be worried sick, as it must be going on three days since her kidnapping. She also knew she was in the cabin to which she'd been brought the night before, spacious but sparsely furnished.

Then she heard it, a soft buzzing sound. For a moment, she closed her eyes to pretend she was home in England, in the Bedfordshire countryside watching bees alight upon the flowers. It took her a second to realize someone was snoring close by. Opening her eyes again, she lifted her head and saw a man at the other end of the cabin where there was a table and chairs.

Good. Snoring meant sleeping, which meant the possibility of escape. For even though she'd been terrified and tired when rescued from the Chinese ship, she recalled her rescuer saying he was *not* in the queen's navy. Thus, she was probably on another pirate ship.

Her hope now was for it to be docked. Otherwise, she would tear off the already ripped and ruined gown and swim for shore, if it was within sight.

What choice did she have?

Swinging her legs off the bed, Beryl put her feet to the floor and stood. Instantly, with a feeling of lightheaded unsteadiness, she sank back down. It wasn't the rocking of the ship affecting her so much as the lack of food and the long hours on the junk with her heart pounding and terror being her constant companion.

The man who'd escorted her to the cabin the evening before, a soft-spoken, red-bearded sailor, had given her water when asked. Her mouth again dry and the dizziness remaining, she wanted more water, as well as to relieve herself and desperately hoped there was some option better than a chamber pot.

Drats! It was hard to think of how to escape when one wanted both to have a drink and to use the privy!

More slowly, Beryl stood again and, lifting her bedraggled skirts so she didn't trip, began to creep across the cabin. Of course, the door had to be on the other side of the snoring man, whom she now recognized as the captain who'd taken her from the pirate junk.

The cabin was longer than it was wide, and holding her breath as if it would make her smaller and quieter, she had nearly gone by him when his arm shot out and grabbed her wrist.

Captured again!

CHAPTER TWO

"*A*hhheeee," Beryl shrieked, pulling hard to get away. "Unhand me," she demanded at once to the crone who'd attacked her.

To her surprise, he let her go so quickly she went crashing to the cabin wall.

Instantly, he stood up. "Are you injured?"

She shook her head. She'd simply had the wind knocked out of her and been given another fright to pile upon all the other frights she'd experienced, that was all. She was starting to hate traveling. More than once, she wished she were back in England with her mother and five younger brothers and sisters. Even if she left for home tomorrow, it would be months before she reached London.

"Where do you think you're going?" the captain asked.

Shrugging, she told him the first thought in her head, "To find a privy."

His eyebrows shot up, dark brows on a tanned face, under very dark hair, which was too long for civilized company. She would have said it was black if they were in England. But here, amongst the Chinese with their shiny ebony hair, she would say the captain's was the deepest, richest brown.

His eyes were also extremely dark, but they were not unkind. Moreover, he spoke her language, so pirate or not, she ought to count herself better off than she'd been the day before.

"Immediately," she added, feeling her cheeks heat up.

His eyes widened. Perhaps it was the first time a woman had uttered those words on board his ship.

"Of course," he said. Then he gestured to a narrow door she hadn't noticed. "Luckily, I have my own. It's rather rudimentary, but my crew use a hole next to the bowsprit, so . . ."

If she took his meaning correctly, she had better not complain, or she would be on deck looking for the mysterious bowsprit.

"I'll leave you in private," he offered, which she thought was more than generous. "Just tap on the cabin door when you're finished, and I'll come back in."

"Am I a prisoner, then?"

He took her measure with his dark eyes. "No, Miss Angsley, but you are female and beautiful, and on a ship of men, some of whom haven't *cracked Jenny's tea cup* in a while, if I may be so blunt."

He could be blunt because it took her a long moment to understand it was a fancy way of saying . . . *oh!* She understood it was nothing to do with drinking tea or cracking fine porcelain.

Her cheeks grew hotter. Moreover, he'd called her beautiful. He wasn't such a bad pirate after all, despite his uncombed hair and his unshaved cheeks giving him a rakish air.

"It would be best," he continued, "if you remain in my cabin until we decide what to do with you."

What to do with her? Beryl wanted to discuss it at once except she could wait not an instant longer. With a curt nod, she hurried to the privy and closed herself in.

A few minutes later, feeling much relieved if a little mortified, she reentered the captain's cabin. He seemed to be trying to protect her, but she would feel better if she had a weapon of her own.

Glancing around, she noticed his gun on the table but shivered. *How would she ever figure out how to use it?*

There was also a sword, but she couldn't imagine running someone through or slicing them. She'd seen both last night on the deck of the junk as her rescuer led her away, and the terrible scenes had replayed in her dreams all night long.

Spying a candlestick, she snatched it up. This was more like it. Made of brass, she could hold it by the long end and give someone a good bashing on the head with the heavy base.

Practicing, Beryl swung it around a few times. Yes, it would work if she could only conceal it somehow.

Giving it another try, she raised the candleholder overhead. As the door opened, she turned.

"What in blue blazes are you doing?" The captain was carrying a tray of food, and she slowly lowered the candlestick, replacing it on the table.

"I was protecting myself."

His face broke out into a grin, and her breath hitched. He was handsome already, but when he smiled, he was gorgeous.

"Are you a pirate?" she asked without preamble.

"No, Miss Angsley. I am a privateer, meaning I have a letter of marque from the queen herself."

"Why aren't you in the Royal Navy?"

He set the tray down next to the candlestick, pushing a large tin out of the way.

"Not that it's any of your business, but if I were in the Royal Navy, I certainly wouldn't be a captain, and the pay is not nearly as good."

He grinned again, showing her his teeth, which she noted looked well cared for.

"Are you hungry?" he asked.

"Yes, very much so." Before she could inspect the tray, a flash of orange rushed in through the open door, ran around the long cabin, jumped onto the bed before jumping down again, and finally came over to rub against her legs.

"I wondered where you were," the captain addressed the rather short-legged cat. Then he looked at Beryl. "I wasn't really wondering at all, just humoring him."

She nodded. *Humoring a cat?* Maybe the man was insane from too much saltwater. She'd heard that could be a problem. There was only one other chair at the table besides the one he'd vacated, and as she approached it, the captain pulled it out for her.

A gentleman, she thought. Before she could draw the food toward her, however, the cat sprung onto her lap.

"*Oh!*" she exclaimed as he looked up at her, his golden-eyed glance locking with her own. What could she do but stroke him from his soft head down along his sturdy body toward his absurdly fluffy tail?

"That's a first," the captain muttered.

"What is?" She continued as the animal began to purr loudly.

"Leo is usually a bit standoffish."

Shrugging, she couldn't explain it. She had never had a special way with animals, nothing out of the ordinary. Not like her best friend, Eleanor, who positively glowed when surrounded by ducks and sheep, or whatever else she found in nature.

However, gratifying as it was to be honored by the cat, Beryl was famished and, at last, pulled the tray close.

"Not to be rude, but what is that?" She pointed to what looked like a cracker only thicker and grayer.

"That's there to scare you," the captain said, and she stared at him.

"Only jesting, Miss Angsley. We have no bread as it spoils too quickly. That's hardtack, like a dry, tasteless biscuit, only good for dunking in soup or keeping your teeth scraped and cleaned, but it is filling. Under here, however," and he lifted a cloth from over the other dishes, "this should be more recognizable. Cook's best porridge and eggs."

"Eggs? But how—"

"We have hens on board."

Nodding, with her stomach growling loudly enough to drown out the orange cat's purr, Beryl couldn't say another word until she'd eaten. Tucking into the meal, she noticed the captain resume his seat and also take one of the two mugs of tea off the tray.

It was certainly not like the first-rate dining she'd had upon the Royal Navy vessel on which she and her father had sailed from England. It didn't matter. As she swallowed bite after bite, she started to feel better.

When she'd devoured every last morsel, trying not to drop any onto the cat's head—and failing—she then reached for the tea.

"Shoo," the captain said. "Go on, you moggy." He reached over and gave the cat a shove so he jumped down. Leo paused only long enough to hiss at him before jumping onto the bed, curling up, and going to sleep.

"He doesn't seem to like you," she observed.

The captain shrugged. "He's only mine by default."

She waited, but he said no more on that matter, so she decided to focus on a more important one.

"Where are we docked?"

"We are anchored, not docked, in the Tunglung channel, specifically in what we call Rocky Bay."

"Is it terribly dangerous?" she asked, pausing in sipping the tea, which was delicious—naturally, since they were in the heart of the tea-growing Far East.

"Do you mean because of the rocks or the opium smugglers?" the captain asked. Shrugging before she could answer, he added. "The answer is yes either way, but we know where the rocks are, and we can outrun or overpower most smugglers. The candlestick wouldn't help you in either case."

"The candlestick is not for what's surrounding this ship. It's for what's on it. I have no idea whether I've gone from a bad situation to a worse one." She got to the point. "If you are not a pirate, I take it I am not a prisoner. Will you set me ashore?"

He paused, which she didn't think was a good sign.

"That depends. What are you doing in China, or the Great Qing Kingdom as they call it here? And don't tell me you were trying to force your British religion on these people. They are just fine as Buddhists or Confuscists, or any number of other beliefs. They don't need—"

"There is no 'British religion,' Captain," Beryl cut in. "In any case, I'm not a missionary. I'm a diplomat's daughter. Since the Treaty of Nanking, you must be aware the queen sends her representatives back and forth all the time, especially with the Qing emperor always grumbling about the treaty's terms. I came over on a royal warship, with my father and a handful of other diplomats to soothe things over."

"You say the word *diplomat* as if it were magical," he remarked. "Yet there has been much bloodshed before *and* after diplomats have done their work."

She frowned at him. *Was he insulting her father?* She wasn't sure.

He sipped his tea, looking thoughtful. "If only people would stop dumping things into harbors—first the Americans with our tea in Boston and then the Qing's administrator with our opium in the Canton harbor. This tossing away of British goods only brings the might of the crown down upon the perpetrators."

"I don't know about Canton, Captain, but the Americans seemed to have done just fine after tossing our tea into the Atlantic waters."

"True, but if the Chinese had done as well, would you need to arrive in a fully armed British warship?"

"Your point is taken." Though she knew the warship was for her safety and that of the diplomats on board, she hadn't thought about why they needed to be kept safe or from whom.

"Shall we go back to the facts I am familiar with? I set foot on dry land a little over two months ago at Stanley—am I close to Stanley?" she asked, interrupting herself.

He shook his head.

"We then went overland to Victoria Town in the north of the Hong Kong Island. Am I close to Victoria?" she asked again.

Once more, he shook his head.

Her father must be frantic. "We've spent two months in China. My father met with many Manchu administrators, and we even went together to the mainland to Peking. I saw The Forbidden City from the outside. Have you seen it?" she asked him.

"No. I haven't seen much beyond the coasts."

What a shame, she thought, and told him so. "My father went inside the palace to visit with members of the Manchus. It was so beautiful. Recently, we traveled to Nanjing in the Jiangsu province because of the Taiping Rebellion. You've heard of it?"

He nodded.

"Our queen thought perhaps a British diplomat could help prevent bloodshed, as you mentioned."

"You mean Queen Victoria's advisors want to keep the country stable for the Manchus so Britain doesn't lose any ground in its opium trade. A civil war could cause a disruption in the selling of opium to the Chinese people."

Was that what all this was about? For her, it had simply been an opportunity to spend time with her father and buy first-rate silk and perfume, unlike anything her friends had back home. Moreover, she was enjoying her last months of freedom before marriage to her viscount. Rather, she *had* been enjoying it until she'd been kidnapped.

"Naturally, we went by coastal route to Nanjing, because of the Taiping marching all over the place. It was safer. I believe my father thinks it a lost cause and will take news back to the queen that war is imminent among the Chinese peoples. We'd only just arrived back on Hong Kong Island a few days ago. I barely got to feel the earth stop rolling beneath me when I was plucked off the street in plain sight of the British soldiers, or would've been if it hadn't been black as pitch."

"Why was it so dark?" he asked.

"Because I had a sack over my head, of course" *Wasn't he listening to her tale of abduction?* "Next thing, I knew, I was in some kind of wagon and then on a small boat, I think two men were rowing, and then I was lugged aboard the Chinese junk where you found me. We're supposed to be going home today, or maybe it was yesterday."

"You've had quite an adventure, Miss Angsley. I'm glad to know your father is close, probably looking for you along with half the Royal Navy. We'll sail to Stanley Harbor and put you ashore there. I doubt your father has left the area with you missing."

"That would be most welcome, Captain. I just realized I don't even know your name."

"Captain Philip Carruthers, at your service."

She set her mug down on the table.

"Could it be possible you are related to the Carruthers family who lost a son in a carriage accident? It seems too strange a coincidence if you are."

She noticed his jaw had gone slack.

CHAPTER THREE

Philip stood slowly. He'd come fourteen thousand miles in order never to be reminded of his brother's fatal accident. Except, of course, for Leo.

She flinched, and he realized he was leaning over her. Pivoting, he walked the length of his cabin, which only took about six long strides and brought him to his bedside.

Staring down at the cat, Robert's cat, he let the buzzing in his ears quiet before he turned to her.

"Strange as the coincidence may be, Miss Angsley, somehow you do know of my family and our painful past. However, I have no wish to discuss it."

"Very well," she conceded. "We'll discuss it no more."

She sipped her tea again, draining the mug and even eyeing the bottom as if hopeful for more. He would bring more blasted tea in order to escape the room where suddenly Robert had been conjured.

In any case, the blasted woman was as chatty as a magpie. He'd just managed to stop her long rambling tale of a few months in China, only to find out she knew his family in England. However, he doubted she could hold her tongue, since she hadn't stopped waggling it since she'd opened her eyes.

Sure enough, she spoke again.

"I offer my condolences, for it appears you grieve still."

His grief was his own damned business. "Thank you for your sympathy, as long as we speak no more of it."

"Of course not," she said, pushing her chair away from the table and standing. "I completely understand."

As she approached him, looking entirely uncooperative, he would have backed up if he could, but there was nowhere to go.

"Certainly, we will not speak another word about it," she repeated.

Reaching out, she stroked his brother's cat on the head. If he'd dared to attempt the same, he would have pulled back a scratched and bleeding hand. Leo seemed to like her, though, purring happily.

Traitor, he thought, looking at the animal which stretched languorously under her touch. *Didn't he have mice or rats to catch down below?*

"Yes, I believe we have come to an understanding," he agreed, "that we will not."

Eyeing him, she nodded.

"Except I thought only to tell you how my family was touched by the terrible incident, too," she added, "not that I shall tell another word of it."

And she didn't. She pursed her lips and caressed his cat, and even sat again on his bed, saying nothing except a few murmurs of endearment toward Leo.

Philip stared at her. Despite wearing a tattered gown, despite her once fancy-dressed hair having come undone so she had two loose braids hanging down her back, despite a little grime on her face, she was, as he'd said before, a beautiful woman.

And she was being purposefully infuriating.

Sighing, he had to ask, as she likely knew he would.

"All right, tell me how my brother's death touched your family. And be quick about it. I must get on deck."

She eyed him. "If you're sure you want to hear."

Gritting his teeth, he nodded.

"My cousin is John Angsley, the Earl of Cambrey," she stated.

"Cambrey," he repeated, instantly picturing the face of the man Robert's carriage had hit, the very instant his brother died.

"I see. In truth, I am not sure I recalled his surname, thinking of him only as Lord Cambrey."

She nodded. "Of course. Are you aware my cousin was gravely injured, with a broken leg and arm and a terrible blow to his skull?"

Philip nodded. "I was. I even spoke with him before I left England."

Her eyes widened. Apparently, she didn't know that.

She also didn't know he had nearly done something so foul it was worthy of any black-hearted pirate. He'd thought to exact revenge for his brother's death by ruining the earl's fiancée. At the time, he'd been so angry and wounded in his spirit, he wanted to punish someone, anyone, for the loss of his brother—his twin.

Luckily, he'd realized he was in a red haze of misplaced fury *before* he did something unforgiveable. Besides, the earl's lady was a kind woman with whom Philip had thought himself more likely to become smitten than be able to harm.

"So, you are the earl's cousin?" he mused "Quite a bit younger, are you not?"

Nodding again, she said only, "About a decade, in fact, but it's not polite to discuss a woman's age."

Probably true although he was out of practice with what was polite.

"I'll see about getting you more tea." Allowing himself as wide a berth as possible given the circumstances of the close confines, he moved past her and headed to the door.

"Am I to be kept in this cabin then, Captain? I thought you said I wasn't a prisoner. I would very much like some fresh air."

"There is always the porthole, Miss Angsley. They open easily enough. Just don't get your head stuck in one."

With that, he left her. It was first light, and some crew members were swabbing the decks, others checking the sails for rips. A clipper was only as fast as her taut and trim sails, after all. He would fetch more tea, like a bloody servant, but only after conferring with Rufus over the best course of action. They'd started this endeavor two years earlier—two Brits seeking fortune and adventure—and he trusted his first mate and friend from boarding school above all others.

Philip found him on the poop deck, seated on an old wooden tea container and drinking coffee.

"How's the woman?" Rufus asked upon seeing him.

"Hungry, thirsty, spirited, extremely talkative, and no worse for being captured and held on a junk."

"You know their code," his first mate remarked.

Because of the famed and powerful lady pirate, Ching Shih, who'd died only a half-dozen years earlier, the Chinese pirates treated female captives with care. Far better, Philip would guess, than what a woman, especially a lovely one like Miss Angsley, would experience from British pirates, not that there were many around anymore, certainly not in these waters.

In the Orient, there were no true English pirates flying their flags of doom and terror, not like the famed Poseidon's Legion whose stories he'd heard from childhood. Nowadays, it seemed everyone was *behaving* like a pirate, smuggling opium, selling to corrupt Chinese officials, and raiding merchant ships filled with Chinese goods heading to England. Even the Royal Navy assisted the opium trade on behalf of Britain, though the Manchu government still considered the drug forbidden.

"Her father is here on the queen's business," he told Rufus.

"Rather like us, then."

"Probably not. As a diplomat, her father is undoubtedly a tried-and-true believer in turning all of China into docile opium addicts. It has been immensely profitable, after all."

Their own mission was different. Recovering the duchess's necklace was crucial since it was practically a matter of state. That it had been stolen at all was a court disaster because everyone and everything should be safe at Buckingham Palace.

Chinese officials of the Qing Dynasty had been in the palace speaking with the foreign secretary, Lord Palmerston, about the treaties, which the Manchus considered vastly unfair—and then the blasted necklace had gone missing.

Unable to accuse them outright, the queen's foreign affairs minister needed a privateer to retrieve it *without* offending the Chinese. For though the British had soundly defeated the Qing in the first so-called Opium War, they now worked together to rid the waters of Chinese and Japanese pirates who interfered greatly with British merchants.

Luckily, Philip had needed something tangible and difficult to do after Robert's death. His father, who had a royal appointment as the queen's wool supplier, took Philip with him to the palace, and before he knew it, he was captaining his own ship bound for the Orient.

"What are we doing with *her?*" Rufus's gaze went from surveying the ship's decks and the quiet waters around the *Robert* to locking onto Philip's face.

"Her father may be in Stanley, so I suppose we head there."

"Will delay our trip home," his first mate pointed out. "The crew is eager to see the shores of England."

"Do they know I have the necklace?" Philip asked.

"Hard to keep such a thing a secret, Captain, but for now, it's only a rumor. You went on the junk with a sack. You came off the junk with the sack *and* a woman. When your steward cleans your cabin, I imagine he's been paid by half the crew to look in the bag and see what's inside."

There had been a lot of false leads and many dangerous boardings trying to track the necklace, until a tavern in Ningbo and a loose-lipped, opium-addicted pirate mentioned the jewels.

"You may have a day before the hands know for sure, but when they do, they're going to want to set sail for home immediately."

Philip agreed with that entirely. The sooner the *Robert* got underway for Britain, the sooner he and his men got paid. Moreover, the danger of reprisal would increase daily. As more tongues wagged about the necklace having been found, in Bias Bay of all places, more pirates would be on his tail. If not Chui-A-poo, then Shap-ng-tsai. The French might want to reclaim it for their so-called prince-president, Napoleon's nephew, since the jewels had originally belonged to Marie Antoinette. Or even the American pirate, Eli Boggs, might show up.

Philip shuddered, not liking the idea of being cut to bits and sent to the mainland bucket by bucket, which Eli favored as a particularly gruesome warning. *The cruel bastard!*

"We could turn the necklace over to the queen's officials in Victoria Town," Rufus said.

Philip paused and stared at his first mate. Then the man cracked a smile, and they both shared a long and hearty laugh. As if they would trust anyone except each other in this godforsaken land.

"Weigh anchor. We sail for Stanley Bay."

"Aye, aye, Captain."

Then Philip sighed. "I'm going to fetch our unwanted guest a mug of tea."

"Too late," Rufus said, gesturing with a nod behind him.

He turned. Sure enough, on the quarter deck below, Miss Angsley stood, looking almost regal if not for her rags. *Blimey!*

BERYL HELD THE CANDLESTICK in her right hand, keeping it down and concealed in the folds of her skirts. She felt better for holding it as she encountered one crewman after another, stopping, staring, smirking, silent. She wished she'd stayed in the captain's cabin after all but was now fearful of turning her back on any of these men. Since they weren't wearing uniforms of Her Majesty's Navy, they certainly looked like pirates to her.

One laid down his mop and approached her.

"Um." She licked her lips and saw him stare interestedly at her mouth. "Where is Captain Carruthers?" she asked.

Then the sailor's eyes darted lower to her feet, where Leo had suddenly shown himself, having left the cabin with her.

"Sink me!" he exclaimed, looking at her with a newfound admiration. "Have you tamed that vicious beast?"

Eyes wide, he glanced from the cat to her face, then to his right where she now saw the captain descending a small flight of steps, almost a ladder, to the deck she was on. His expression was clearly one of displeasure.

"Thank you," she said to the sailor, who, without another word, quickly returned to his mopping.

Just then, she heard another voice yell out orders to weigh the anchor, and a general flurry of activity ensued.

As soon as he was close enough for her to hear him, the captain said, "I thought I ordered you to remain in my cabin."

"Did you?" she asked. *Had he?* She thought it was more of a suggestion than anything. "I thought I was not a prisoner. On the ship on the way over from England, I was allowed freedom to walk the decks without fear. Don't you have command over your crew?"

She watched his jaw tighten.

"Name?" he asked.

"I beg your pardon?"

"The name of the ship. You spent many months on it. I assume you know its name."

"*Wellesley*," she said.

He nodded. "Quite a bit larger than this one, wouldn't you say? Nice cabin, dining room, good food?"

"Yes," she agreed.

"The *HMS Wellesley* is a Cornwallis Class warship with seventy-four guns, and the men are kept extremely busy running her. My men sometimes have too much time on their hands." He glanced to where the sailor had been swabbing the deck and had now disappeared, caught up in the order, she guessed, to get the ship moving.

In fact, all around her, activity had sprung up, putting the lie to his words.

He followed her glance. "You've given us a task this morning, Miss Angsley. We're heading to Stanley Bay in search of your father."

"Thank you."

They both looked down as Leo circled her hem again and then darted off.

"He keeps the vermin down," Captain Carruthers told her.

She supposed a cat on a ship was a good idea. "How long will the journey take?"

"Not long. We are smaller than the *Wellesley*, but a hell of a lot faster, as you'll find out."

Hm. He might not be a pirate, but he was rude. In any case, she was fairly certain a privateer *was* a pirate, except with some official papers. He could still get up to no good and into trouble.

Thinking of trouble, when a voice spoke close behind her, she whirled around, raising the brass candlestick without thinking.

"What the devil?" she heard the captain exclaim as she faced a sailor with wide, startled eyes. Then a moment later, Captain Carruthers ordered her to "Lower your weapon!"

She could hear the amusement in his voice.

"Report, Bantam," he said to the sailor.

The man still stared at her but addressed his captain. "I checked the tye, tack, brace, and stays, Captain, and the robands are all secure."

"Good. Have Churley find someone to relieve Jack in the crow's nest."

The sailor had plainly been given an order but remained standing there, gawking at her. She began to feel like a rare specimen, indeed.

"See to it," the captain urged. "Smartly now, hurry along. Jack's been up there five hours, I think."

At last, the crewman moved. "Aye, Captain." And he dashed away.

"Another reason for you to stay in my cabin? Not only is it safer for you, it's safer for all of us. My crew will be so distracted by you if you remain on deck, they'll be leaving lines loose or untied altogether."

Then he frowned at the "weapon" in her hand.

"If I take you to the galley where we make tea, will you give me back my candlestick?"

She felt her cheeks heat up.

He held out his hand.

Like a child who'd taken something not belonging to her, Beryl handed it to him, then followed him to the galley, where she met the cook, a gruff-looking man with an even gruffer voice, who could strangely make a perfect pot of tea.

"In any case, there's nowhere for you to go as comfortable as my cabin," the captain told her. "Therefore, you might as well return to it until we reach Stanley."

Beryl decided he was right. She'd seen enough of the Hong Kong coastline to last a lifetime, so she returned to his cabin with her tea. Soon, she hoped to be seeing the familiar sight of Stanley Bay again, and the Royal Naval vessel that would take her home.

CHAPTER FOUR

"**O**f all the damn nuisances!" Philip exclaimed when they reached Stanley and there was no ship belonging to Her Majesty's Navy.

"They wouldn't up and leave her, would they?" he muttered to Rufus as they explored the harbor.

Maybe if they cherished a moment's silence, they would, Philip thought unkindly. He'd checked on Miss Angsley once during the quick voyage and had to back out of the cabin while she was still talking.

Maybe she was simply nervous. Or maybe he'd forgotten how women behaved since he hadn't been in the company of one for a long while. At least, not the kind of company that wasn't paid for and was handled nearly in silence except for a few grunts and moans. The Chinese whores had been very kind to him and his men whenever he'd granted shore leave or taken the opportunity himself. Delicate and bawdy at the same time, speaking only enough English to haggle over the price.

Regardless, he knew every man aboard the *Robert* would trade a week of enjoying the skillful harlots of Shanghai in order to get home to England sooner. They needed to get underway within a couple weeks or risk foul weather when they rounded the southern tip of Africa. The Cape of Good Hope cared for no man's schedule!

They'd scoured the harbor and even hailed two English merchant ships but were told the same thing—the only Royal Naval ship had left the day before. He sent Rufus and another crewman ashore in a rowboat to suss out any information about her father, Lord Harold Angsley, and then he knocked on the door of his cabin to tell her the bad news.

"Come in," she said.

He smiled to himself. She did sound like a privileged English miss. Basically, she sounded like home to him, and he yearned to be on his way back.

Pushing the door gently open, his eyes found her seated at his table, perusing the charts he'd left upon it. There had probably been little else for her to do though he was certain he had a few books stowed away in one of his drawers.

She looked up at him with pretty brown eyes, and he felt a pang of something. *Admiration? Attraction? Desire?*

She'd taken some time to wash up. Her face was clean, and she'd somehow, in the magical way of females, put her hair up again. Pins such as he'd had the privilege to pull out of a few English ladies' finely dressed hair, releasing their tresses, had probably been lurking in her hair all along, under the braids.

He was rather sorry to see her appearing so polished, in fact. He'd already spent a moment or two imagining her hair out of the plaits altogether and running his fingers through her silky waves.

Avast! he cautioned himself. Remember her social status. Miss Beryl Angsley was a young lady traveling with her father, a member of the aristocracy, and thus, most assuredly, a virgin.

"I looked out the porthole, Captain," she said by way of greeting, "being careful not to get my head stuck, of course."

She had a sense of humor, too.

"What did you see?" he asked.

"I believe I recognize Stanley Bay. Am I correct?"

"You are." *How did he tell her the awful truth? That her ship had sailed without her. He would put it off, that's how.*

"When you first docked here, months ago, where did you stay?"

Cocking her head, she recalled, "In rooms in Stanley Fort. Not for long, though. Soon, we went to—"

He interrupted before she regaled him with another story of her travels in China. "Is that where your father is staying?"

"Yes, that's where I was when I was kidnapped." She got up and went to a porthole. "I'm sure it's that building on the right."

Facing him, she said, "Please, Captain, won't you take me ashore so I can find him."

If only it were so easy.

He considered where the Royal Navy and her father might have gone looking for her. With the size of China, Lord Angsley must have found it a daunting notion.

"Captain, will you take me ashore now?" she repeated.

Hearing footsteps on deck, he knew his men had returned. A couple moments later, Rufus appeared in the passageway.

"Anything?"

A curt shake of his head, and then he indicated Philip should follow him out of the cabin.

Miss Angsley frowned. "Is anything wrong, Captain?"

Maybe everything. "I'll return in a moment."

"Well?" Philip asked as soon as he closed the cabin door.

Rufus shrugged. "No sign of a party of diplomats. As you know, nearly everyone is English or speaks English on the island, and everyone is talking about the kidnapping of an aristocrat's daughter, including all our hands, who now know whom they've got on board. And colonists are up in arms because it happened on the island, on British territory."

"Do they know who did it?"

Rufus raised an eyebrow. "Meaning, might they think *we* did it if they find out she's on board?"

Philip grunted. "I'm fairly certain we can talk our way out of that, or at least she can explain. But we certainly don't want them searching the *Robert*, do we?"

Not only the duchess's jewels but a few other prized possessions had found their way into his ship's hold, to be sold back in Britain. All of it ill-gotten gain removed from Chinese pirate junks. The Royal Navy wouldn't hesitate to confiscate the lot.

"The sooner we get rid of her, the better," Rufus said.

"Agreed," though it caused him a moment's discontent to think of never seeing her or her soft brown eyes again.

"I will escort her ashore myself and check in at the barracks office to find out about her father's whereabouts."

"And leave her safely in their keeping?" Rufus asked, frowning. "You will leave her, won't you?"

Philip stayed silent. *If the Royal Navy and her father had left her behind, how could he do the same?*

"You feel responsible for her, don't you, Lord Corsair?" Rufus guessed, offering a lopsided grin.

Philip cringed as he always did when one of his crew called him that. It was a ridiculous moniker, a jest they'd come up with over too much rum when first leaving British waters.

"You know the rule—save a life, keep a life," Philip reminded him.

"She should be in debt to you for the rest of her life, but you shouldn't feel responsible forever. It's a stupid rule."

Philip shrugged. "No rowboat for Miss Angsley. Take us to the dock."

With that, he returned to his cabin. She looked up with those trusting eyes.

"As soon as we're docked, I'll take you ashore."

"Thank you, Captain."

"Seeing as you don't have anything with you, I suppose you're ready to disembark. That is, if you'll leave my candlestick alone."

She smiled at him.

There was nothing more to say. No point he could see to telling her he feared her father and their party had left. She would find that out soon enough.

Within a few minutes, he was assisting her off his ship and onto one of the docks in Stanley Bay, and they were on the rudimentary street. There had been little habitation in Stanley, or any of Hong Kong Island, until the British took control and colonized it nine years earlier. It still wasn't much to look at, but they strolled through the port until they reached the barracks.

"This is where I was," she exclaimed. "And I strolled down that way," she paused to point past the barracks to the far tip of the cove, "when I was set upon."

It made the hair on the back of his neck stand up. Miss Angsley should have been safe here of all places, surrounded by British officers, unless someone had wanted her in particular. Someone who could take her quickly to the next cove, then onto a rowboat to a pirate junk. Someone powerful like Chui-A-poo.

"No matter, Miss Angsley." He patted his revolver on his hip, confident six shots would be enough to protect them both. "Let's see about getting you reunited with your father."

They soon found the barracks, and from the first sailor they encountered, they learned precisely what Philip's first mate had thought—the diplomats, including Lord Angsley, and the *HMS Wellesley* had departed.

All the spark seemed to go out of Miss Angsley. Fearing she might faint, he tucked her arm under his, and they continued walking toward the ensign's office as if they were promenading along Pall Mall.

"So, what do I do with you, Beryl?" Philip asked, his tone light so as not to frighten her. She was in quite a predicament.

"If you don't mind, Captain, I think I am ready to go home."

She said it as if they were at one end of Hyde Park, and she wanted him merely to drive her in his carriage around to Kensington Gardens at the other end. Not sail across to the other side of the world.

"Let's see if anyone has any more information. The ensign of the barracks will probably know something."

At seeing her, the young ensign's eyes bugged out of his head, and he jumped up from his chair.

"Thank the good Lord!" he said. Then he frowned and confirmed what they already knew.

Hearing Lord Angsley had left already did not sound any better the second time.

Philip felt Beryl's entire body begin to tremble, and quickly, he settled her in a chair.

"My father would not leave me behind," she protested, her voice thick with emotion.

"No, Miss Angsley. Not by choice," the ensign assured her. "Lord Angsley was beside himself with agitation. The *Wellesley* has left Stanley but not yet China. They are in search of you. They've headed to Dianbai."

"Dianbai?" Philip exclaimed. "They went west?"

The ensign stood up taller. "And who are you, sir?"

"Captain Carruthers. I'm the man who rescued her about three hours *east* of here." Philip had to pace or he was going to explode. "And here she plainly is, Ensign, as you can see. With her father heading a hundred and ninety nautical miles in the wrong direction!"

The ensign's cheeks went slightly red. "We had no way of knowing where she was, but the pirate, Shap-ng-tsai, is hold up there with about seventy junks. We thought perhaps he'd amassed a small fleet because he'd taken her."

"No," Philip told the man. "He didn't take her and he's not there in any case. He's moved his entire damn pirate fleet to Hai Phong."

"I don't know Hai Phong, Captain," the ensign said, speaking more respectfully. "Which part of China?" He started to glance down at the charts on his desk.

"Not China, Ensign. The Kingdom of Việt Nam, or . . . what are they calling it now? The Empire of Đại Nam. I only know because I have had dealings with the villagers near Dianbai, people who've been paying Shap-ng-tsai for years not to raid them. They're not paying anymore because he's gone. As you can imagine, they're happy to talk about it."

"I see." The ensign looked perplexed. "I'm sure the officers on the *Wellesley* have learned this already, as they would have reached Dianbai late yesterday." Then his expression brightened. "You own the clipper that just docked?"

"Aye."

"Then you will take Miss Angsley to Hai Phong and reunite her with her father."

Philip already knew he was going to do so, had known it the instant the ensign mentioned Lord Angsley's westerly destination, but he didn't like to be told.

"I do not work for the navy. However, my vessel is for hire. How much will Her Majesty pay me for my trouble?"

Beryl, who had been unusually quiet during the exchange, suddenly interrupted.

"You *are* a pirate. I knew it. Only a pirate would demand restitution for such as this."

Philip glanced at the ensign, feeling a moment's nervousness. He was, after all, in a Royal Naval barracks surrounded by armed men who didn't look too fondly on pirates.

"I am a privateer, as I've told you." He looked at the ensign. "I have a letter of marque from Her Majesty Queen Victoria, but it doesn't charge me with delivering irresponsible females who get themselves kidnapped by wandering alone out of the safety of the barracks."

"Oh!" Beryl exclaimed. "Irresponsible? How dare you!"

Philip rolled his eyes. *How dare he?* Again, they were not at a bloody dinner party where he'd spilled wine on the Persian rug.

"I have completed the orders of my queen," he said to the ensign watching their exchange, "and I am heading back to England."

"It is in the same general direction," the ensign pointed out.

Philip bloody well knew it, but that didn't change the matter. Delays were dangerous. Anything could happen, including the *Robert* being blown to smithereens by going near a potential battle between Royal Naval officers and crazed pirates, a battle in which Philip had absolutely no stake.

"I will need compensation," he said once more, fearing the man was too low level to be able to offer him anything, but it never hurt to try.

"What might you have in mind, Captain? Though there's not much I can do, I would dearly love to solve this problem."

The ensign's gaze flickered over to Beryl, and she crossed her arms.

"I am not a problem," she muttered.

Ignoring her, Philip thought a moment. Mr. Churley, his quartermaster, would be thrilled to take on supplies, especially familiar items, rare elsewhere in the Orient, but quite normal here in colonial Hong Kong. Perhaps some custard powder or sultanas, some clotted cream or bacon.

"I could send my quartermaster ashore with a couple crewmen to gather supplies. I'm sure you've got some British delicacies we haven't had for two years. Do you think you could provide us with what we need for our long journey home?"

The man nodded thoughtfully. "I believe I can, Captain. I could not give you coin of the realm, for certain, but I can give you stores."

"Fine then, I'll take Miss Angsley to Hai Phong, and the *HMS Wellesley* had better be there."

The ensign appeared relieved, having done his part to further the reunification of father and daughter.

"And if it isn't there?" Beryl asked, standing up.

Then what? Philip wondered.

CHAPTER FIVE

With their necessary stores aboard the *Robert*, along with three cases of the Royal Navy's favorite Plymouth gin and plenty of limes, they weighed anchor and left Stanley Bay midday with about five hours of light left.

For Miss Angsley's sake, Philip had even procured a gown from an English colonist since, more than once, she'd expressed her discomfort wearing her grubby garment. Philip couldn't believe she was so uncomfortable she couldn't wait a few days until they reached the *Wellesley*. For his part, he had easily become accustomed to wearing the same shirt, trousers, and coat for weeks.

And some of his crew had only one pair of pants!

However, when he saw her emerging from a room on the barracks with a clean dress, he could see it pleased her tremendously, and, for some reason, her happiness lightened his heart.

Moreover, the new gown, which he surmised was nothing like the à la mode fashion in Paris or London, exposed her long graceful neck and the creamy, smooth skin of her décolletage. He doubted it was meant to spark desire, as the woman who'd owned it was the middle-aged wife of a clerk on the island. All the same, its simply cut design displayed more of Miss Angsley than her own fashionably high-necked traveling gown she'd discarded.

For the first time, Philip could see she wore a gold chain with a green pendant. The Chinese pirates would have taken it in an instant if they'd seen it.

She probably hadn't even thought of that. Had she understood how much danger she had been in? He found himself belatedly feeling a little appalled on her behalf at what might have happened.

Miss Beryl Angsley didn't belong here in the Orient, and he thanked the lucky sailor's stars he'd found her in the pirate junk. Even with the Chinese pirates' code, she would have been wedded against her will within days so the pirate captain, or Chui-A-poo if she'd been captured for him, could enjoy her thoroughly.

Now, if he could only get her back on board the *HMS Wellesley*.

DESPITE THE CASES OF gin, Rufus scowled upon seeing his captain return with their unwanted guest. Philip also noticed his first mate's gaze take in the newly revealing gown.

"Trouble," Rufus murmured as Philip sent her immediately to his cabin.

"Trouble," Rufus repeated under his breath when they stood on the quarter deck later, laying out a course for Hai Phong.

Normally, Philip and his first mate would be in his cabin seated at the table. Instead, they'd spread the charts on the deck and were considering any potential dangers.

"Speak of the devil," Philip said as Leo sprang onto the center of the map he was examining, sitting practically on top of their destination.

"You know the cat isn't what I was referring to," Rufus protested.

"No matter. I couldn't leave her here. Who knows how long it would be before the navy finished fighting with Shap-ng-tsai and realized she wasn't captured by him? And what if her father got himself killed? Then what would happen to her?"

Rufus stared at him. Philip stared back.

"What?" he asked finally, but he knew what his first mate was thinking, that he had grown a soft spot for the lady. More likely, he had something hard for the lady rather than soft, considering her shapely figure and kissable mouth.

Kissable mouth?

Pointless yearnings in any case, seeing where they were—in the middle of the China Sea and about to turn her over, with any luck, to the Royal Navy. Undoubtedly, he would never see her again.

Shaking his head, Philip glanced again at the chart, nudging Leo with the toe of his boot until the animal hissed and ran off.

"We could go straight through, be there in about thirty hours."

Rufus shrugged. "Not worth the risk, is it?"

Probably not, Philip thought. Sailing at full speed in the pitch black was a fool's journey. Besides, with the clipper's capabilities, they wouldn't be far behind Lord Angsley when they reached Hai Phong. Maybe they could stop the captain of the *Wellesley* from engaging with the pirates at all.

"We'll try to reach Shangchuan Island tonight, and tuck in at Shadi Bay if we make it that far."

Rufus was still grumbling when he went to give the crew their orders.

Philip tried to ignore the twinge of misgivings he'd had since first seeing Miss Angsley on the junk in Bias Bay. It seemed, though, he was destined to be with her for a couple days longer.

BERYL DECIDED TO ACQUIESCE to the captain's wishes and remain in the cabin. Besides, it was late and growing cold and windy on deck. When she mentioned this to the sailor who brought her some supper on a tray, he laughed.

"The wind is our best friend, miss. Without it, we'd be dead in the water."

She didn't like the way he emphasized the word *dead*. She'd noticed the line of canons on the *Robert*, as the ship was called. She knew it was named for Captain Carruthers' dead brother, which seemed an ill omen. Nevertheless, the weaponry reassured her they weren't relying only on speed to outrun danger. It appeared they could fight if need be.

A scratching at the door alerted her to the cat wanting to enter the cabin, and she opened the door.

"Leo," she greeted when he rubbed around her ankles, able to get close to her legs since she no longer had on her layers of petticoats. Her "new" dress, in pale green silk, was simple but clean, which felt like an absolute luxury. Anywhere else in the world, she knew the plain gown would be made of mere homespun for the woman the captain bought it from was not wealthy by British standards. In China, though, the silk was as cheap as cotton.

Her old dress of cream brocade with blue panels and gold thread, she'd left on the island with the clerk's wife, who was only too happy for the fabric. And as soon as she'd returned to the privacy of the cabin, Beryl had removed her petticoats, stained with seawater. They now lay discarded in a heap in the corner.

After a few moments of letting her rub the top of his head and even under his chin, Leo wandered toward the bed. Beryl was glad of the company, assuming she would be alone until morning. The captain had mentioned books in the small chest of drawers beside the bed, so she followed the cat.

Rummaging through the drawers, she found a small collection of stories by the American Edgar Allan Poe, which she tossed aside as too unsettling. There was also a well-read, thick tome of Shakespeare. However, she settled on a translation of Homer's *Odyssey*, a fitting story for her own strange journey.

Earlier, she'd quite enjoyed perusing the maps on his table, but he'd taken them along with the bag he'd slept beside when he'd first brought her to his ship the night before.

Was it truly only the previous night? It seemed as if it were a lot longer. Moreover, she felt as if she'd been traveling for days, getting nowhere, from the moment the infernal rice sack had been yanked over her head, ruining her impeccably dressed hair.

Captain Carruthers had called her irresponsible, but she'd been only a few yards away from the barracks, and she'd been told Hong Kong Island was safe. *How was she to know pirates lurked about by the shore like water-snakes?*

And then, she hadn't understood a thing anyone had said, until one of the Chinese pirates said "Lady Brit" and later pantomimed they'd been watching her, showing her a spyglass. She supposed she and her father had been visible enough in their travels on the mainland. If someone had taken a liking to her, there wasn't much she could do.

Then the same pirate with the long, tightly braided queue had said, "You make wife," pointing off the junk's deck into the darkness, and her blood had run cold.

Thank God for Captain Carruthers. She didn't fancy gaining a pirate husband if that was what the man meant. What's more, she had a fiancé back home, chosen from the group of perfectly good suitors she'd met during the Season.

When London's social events were winding down, she'd accepted the proposal of Lord Arthur Wharton, only a couple years her senior. He was nice. His family was nice. His manners were nice. He even had a nice horse when they went riding in Hyde Park together. And, of course, he had a very nice yearly income from his father's estate so her parents were pleased.

Thus, even though she'd felt no compunction to marry him when first partnered on the dance floor or at a dinner party, eventually, when faced with another Season, she'd decided she was simply being too fussy. *How could she ask for more than kind, good-looking, and wealthy?* Besides, he'd declared he had great affection for her.

Though as soon as she'd said yes to Arthur, it felt very much like a rice sack was put over her head—now that she knew what that felt like. In order to enjoy a few months of freedom before becoming the Viscountess of Wharton, Beryl had begged her father to let her go with him.

Now, though, after this terrifying excursion, marriage to Arthur was looking more and more desirable.

The vessel was sailing very smoothly, and the sailor who'd left her meal had lit the two lamps. She noticed with a small smile the candlestick had disappeared. Apparently, she was not to be trusted, but she no longer felt she needed it, either. Perhaps it was the fluffy orange cat or perhaps because the captain had bought her a clean dress.

Who would ever believe her outlandish adventure? She hoped her journal, written diligently every single day of her travels, was still safe in her trunk with her father on the *Wellesley*. A lump formed in her throat, thinking of him somewhere up ahead searching for her.

Sipping the wine that came with her meal, Beryl swallowed her sadness, heartened by the knowledge she was even then sailing toward him. What a pity, though, the most exciting part of her travels wouldn't be in her journal. Maybe she should commit her story to paper immediately while she could still recall the scent and rough feel of the horrid rice bag. More than that, she could remember in detail the interior of the Chinese pirate's cabin on the junk, with the ornate teapot on his table and two fancy swords hanging over his bed.

Studying her surroundings, neither overly stark nor luxurious yet comfortable with a few niceties, such as a mantel clock and a washing bowl, she wouldn't be surprised if the captain had writing implements.

Glancing at the cat, her only company, she said, "Tell me, Leo, are there pen and paper here?"

Idly, opening the large tin cannister in the middle of the table, she discovered it contained metal balls. *Strange.* She picked one up, then another, and then gave up trying to decipher their use.

Hoping the captain wouldn't mind, she decided to search the cabin for what she desired. She'd already retrieved books from the small dresser and had seen no paper, not even a journal the captain was keeping. There wasn't too much other furniture beyond a trunk, the table at which she sat, and a small wardrobe.

Opening the latter, she found a few thick sweaters and a couple pairs of pants, and not much else. Unfortunately, nothing to write on or with.

Shrugging, Beryl turned to the chest, but, to her dismay, it had a padlock on its latch.

Hmm. She supposed she could ask for paper, but it was hardly worth going on deck this late. She could wait until morning, for as she understood it, she would be on the *Robert* for another two days. For now, she would read the *Odyssey*, quell her curiosity over the trunk's contents, and keep company with the cat.

PHILIP NEARLY WENT TO his cabin half a dozen times— simply to check on Miss Angsley—but then it was too late. She would be asleep, and he didn't wish to awaken her. Indeed, he could think of no believable reason to do so.

Except he rather liked talking to her. It must be the general longing for home and all she represented. True, the choice to miss home had been his own. He'd left England of his own accord, seeking to drive out the sorrow over his twin's futile and senseless death.

Robert's reckless carriage racing had spilled out of Hyde Park onto Oxford Street, and right into the unfortunate Earl of Cambrey, who also very nearly lost his life that day. Trying to avoid the earl's vehicle, as witnesses said, Philip's twin had overturned his carriage, dying instantly when his head struck the street. His lifeless body was dragged until his horses stopped.

And his brother had been considered the responsible one.

Philip didn't take his own ease and find a bunk until the *Robert* was safely anchored in Shadi Bay. Though darkness had overtaken them, still, they'd made it to the southwest side of Shangchuan Island.

And they would leave as soon as there was a hint of dawn creeping over the horizon, and sail all day with the light, perhaps eleven-and-a-half hours.

Confident the lookout would keep a keen eye on the sea around them, Philip fell into a deep slumber as soon as he lay down.

When he was awakened the next morning by the boatswain's whistle, he realized he'd slept in. The sun had already crested the horizon, and by the feel of the vessel beneath his boots as he swung his legs off the bunk, Rufus had weighed anchor and left Shangchuan Island behind.

Thinking kindly on his trustworthy and capable crew, Philip went on deck, still rubbing the crick in his neck and stretching out his back. The first thing he saw was Miss Angsley amongst a huddle of sailors.

Exactly what he didn't want to see—*her* surrounded by drooling crewmen!

She was seated on a closed hatch with a mug of tea in her hand, as if she were in her own drawing room learning the day's gossip. What's more, his men were ignoring their duties and any potential danger.

So much for trustworthy and capable! An entire pirate fleet could come upon them and they wouldn't notice. *Scoundrels, all!*

Philip let out a roar of rage, causing all eyes to settle upon him. Even the blasted cat who was sitting at her feet, looked up. Smarter than his crew, Leo startled, sprang away behind the small deckhouse, and disappeared from sight.

Frozen, his men stared at him as if he were the kraken itself, then taking a hint from the ship's cat, galvanized into action, scattering to their posts.

"Yes, you'd better run," Philip yelled churlishly.

Rufus appeared from the galley, cup of freshly brewed coffee in hand and saw the problem. Instead of looking as annoyed as his captain felt, however, Rufus sent Philip an I-told-you-so smirk and resumed his post on the poop deck at the wheel.

Stalking over to Miss Angsley, the one person who didn't seem at all affected by his outburst, Philip stood before her, blocking the sun from her face.

"Good morning, Captain, and isn't it a lovely one?" She offered him a dazzling smile.

"What do you think you are doing?"

Tilting her head, she asked, "Do you always come upon deck in the morning and create such a fuss? Is bellowing your way of clearing your lungs and getting a good dose of sea air? You made quite an exhilarating sound. I think I shall try it."

She stood up, took a deep breath, and—to his amazement—yelled loudly. Then she laughed, her eyes sparkling in the sunlight.

Was she deranged? Or merely mocking him?

"It does feel good, Captain, I must admit. You've got a grand idea with that." She resumed her seat, mug still in hand. "Perhaps tomorrow, you can get everyone to join in at once. They might be able to hear us back in England."

She *was* mocking him. Undoubtedly.

"I asked you to stay in the cabin," he reminded her, "precisely so you wouldn't distract my crew."

"Pish."

"Pish?"

"Yes, Captain. I was a good guest and stayed in there nearly all of yesterday except for our brief time on shore at Stanley, and I didn't even come out last night when I wanted paper and pen. However, this morning, I decided some sunshine would be lovely."

Was he gaping at her? He felt as if he were. She was simply so engaging and so utterly unusual on board the ship. *Sunshine and paper? Would she demand some wool so she could knit them all caps, too?*

No wonder the men had gathered around her like bees to honey. They wanted to know what she might possibly say or do next. As did he.

As if knowing his thoughts, she surprised him by pointing over his head and behind him.

"What does it say on your pirate flag?"

Philip didn't need to look at the top of the foremast to answer. He flew two flags, a Union Jack and a bright red and yellow pennant with the Carruthers' coat of arms and its motto, *promptus et fidelis.*

"There is no pirate flag," he said through gritted teeth. "As for my family's motto, it translates as *ready and faithful.*"

She was quiet a moment, pondering his words.

"Ready for what and faithful to whom, I wonder," she said at last.

He crossed his arms, although in truth he'd never considered *the what* and *the whom* of it before. He assumed the Carruthers considered themselves ready for anything and faithful to the rest of the family.

"If you will go back to the cabin, I will ask Mr. Churley, my quartermaster, to procure some paper, pen, and ink."

"I will."

Philip sensed she'd agreed too easily. Sure enough, she smiled at him, another rather impressive smile, at that.

"Just as soon as I've finished my tea. Actually, I wouldn't mind another cup if you'd care to join me. Perhaps some more porridge, too."

"This isn't a park in which to have a picnic." He knew he was starting to sound like a prudish governess instead of a bold swashbuckler, but he couldn't help himself. Perhaps because he'd spent two years on his ship with every last soul doing *what* he said, *when* he said it.

And Miss Beryl Angsley was defying him. It couldn't be tolerated, not in front of his men. He had to be firm. He had to show her he ruled his ship with an iron fist.

She gazed up at him, her brown eyes optimistic.

"Another mug of tea," he heard himself agree. "But no porridge!"

⚜

CHAPTER SIX

As Beryl had been told they would, the *Robert* sailed all day until they ran out of light after entering the Qiongzhou Strait. Over a midday meal, the captain kindly pointed it out on a map—a *chart*, he'd called it—which he left with her after she told him she'd enjoyed studying it.

She could see where she'd been and where she was going.

When the captain ate with her midday and explored the charts with her, it was one of the few times she'd spoken with anyone. Except the cat, who visited her every couple of hours until finally settling on the bed at dinner time. By then, she was desperate for company.

Beryl had written down her recollections as soon as Mr. Churley delivered her the pen and paper, and then she had read most of the day apart from when the captain had returned to dine with her again for the evening meal.

Besides discussing the course they were on, he'd told her about his family's country estate in Dumfries, belonging to his father's Scottish side. And then more enthusiastically, he described their modest home in Newquay, Cornwall.

"Merely a house on the bluffs overlooking the harbor," he clarified, "but only a stone's throw from the towns where pirates were purported to have kept their hideouts and even buried their treasure."

It was where he'd spent all his summers and learned to sail on the River Gannel.

His face had lit up with pleasure. "The history of Cornwall always fascinated me as a boy," he confessed.

"Especially the history of pirates, I gather." She could easily picture him as an unruly and inquisitive young lad, maybe because his hair was past his collar and unkempt.

"There were a few caves, which my bro—" he broke off, then after a moment, began again, "My brother and I explored them for hours. However, our little harbor is known mostly for its sardines, not exciting buccaneers and scalawags."

"I've been all the way to the Orient, yet haven't seen any more of Cornwall than traveling by coach to Plymouth where we boarded the *Wellesley*. Nor have I been up to John O'Groats in the north," Beryl confessed.

Strange how she could travel around the world while barely seeing more of Britain than London, Bath, and her family's country home in Bedfordshire. She'd told him about her parents and five siblings, and learned he still had two living siblings, both younger, and how his family now lived mainly in London.

They spoke of everything and nothing, rather freely, as any two people who would soon part and never meet again.

Despite Philip Carruthers being a privateer and a little rough around the edges, which, she supposed, was to be expected on board ship, Beryl liked him immensely. In truth, he'd not simply grown on her, he'd even changed a little—both shaving and combing his hair—perhaps on her account.

While still piratically roguish to her eyes, he was tidy. Moreover, he was extremely interesting, and though overall a serious man, occasionally he made a jest and laughed at his own words. He had a rich laugh and a beautiful smile.

She had no cause to be thinking of Captain Carruthers' smile, she admonished herself. Not while she had a perfectly good fiancé awaiting her return, one with a pleasant smile of his own and also impeccable table manners.

Closing the book, she realized she'd been thinking about the captain again instead of reading. *It wouldn't do.* Tomorrow, *God willing*, she would be reunited with her father by nightfall.

So, what was the point in starting to moon over a dashing sea captain?

Finally, around seven at night, they dropped anchor in the harbor of Haikou, a town she would have dearly loved to explore. To walk on land was now a rare luxury, and would continue to be so until she reached England, months from now, she assumed. In any case, she couldn't actually see the port town, only a few lamps burning. She might as well still be in the middle of the ocean.

Lying down beside Leo as she had done the night before, even though it was still early, sheer boredom sent her off to sleep while petting his soft fur. Nightmarish dreams gave way to Philip Carruthers carrying her on a beach, settling her on the soft sand, and then beginning to chop wood for a fire.

After a few moments, she awakened, realizing the chopping in her dream was knocking at the cabin door. Glancing at the clock, which a sailor had wound each day, she could see it was only a quarter past nine.

"Come in," she called, glad of the company.

The captain entered—the man of her dreams. Seeing her upon his bed, he hesitated, and she felt her cheeks heat up. His hesitation made his entrance seem almost licentious, or, at the very least, inappropriate as if she were undressing or bathing, rather than simply lying down completely clothed.

Nevertheless, rising to a seated position, she gave him a welcoming smile, even as he was backing up a step.

"Do come in, Captain, at least to break the monotony of my evening."

With a curt nod, he took a step inside, considered a moment, and then closed the door behind him.

Her pulse began to trot at such an innocent gesture, obviously done to protect her privacy from the rest of the crew. After all, she'd been alone with him at lunch and again at dinner. However, with the blackness outside the portholes, and only a single lamp lit for her reading, it seemed they were sharing an intimate moment.

If her friends in England could see her now, alone in a man's room—with the man in it!

She nearly giggled out loud with nervousness. Her father and mother would rebuke her for her lack of judgment. However, as she had learned, things were different on a ship.

"I wondered if you might like a nightcap. It is your last evening aboard the *Robert*, after all." He held two empty glasses in his hand.

Having never had a nightcap before, though aware of what it meant, she accepted, and watched while he went to the same wardrobe that held his clothing. Pushing aside the sweaters, he brought out a bottle of brandy, and with a smile, she also noted the missing candlestick.

Turning, he spied her raised eyebrows and gave her his devilishly attractive grin.

"We have gin on board and wine and sometimes rum, but this is the only brandy. It is quite scarce in these parts. Thus, I keep it hidden."

"And you wish to share it with me? I see your bottle is only half full. Is the remainder for your trip home?"

"Exactly," he agreed. "And since we are now heading west, I would say I have begun my trip home."

She watched him pour the amber liquid before realizing she should get off his bed. Extremely glad she hadn't removed her gown to sleep in her chemise, Beryl swung her feet to the floor and stood.

"Will you join me in the dining room, Miss Angsley?" Captain Carruthers asked, gesturing to the small table on which he set the glasses. "You may have my chair as it is the most comfortable."

"Thank you." She took four steps to the 'dining room,' letting him hold the chair for her and push it in before he sat diagonally to her at the small table.

"I'm sorry if you were lonely all day, but we went straight from point A to point B, as it were, in the middle of the sea, with nowhere to hide. Thus, it was all hands on deck in case we met trouble."

She picked up the glass with about an inch of amber liquid, and he did the same.

"I'm glad we didn't meet any trouble," she said. "I've had enough adventure for now. And I thank you for the charts. I was pleased to go back and track my travels."

"You're most welcome." Then he clinked his glass against hers and took a sip, waiting, watching until she did the same.

It burned a little, and Beryl had to fight the urge to cough, but fight it she did. Then she sipped again, and it was much easier the second time. She wouldn't exactly call it delicious, like a glass of madeira, but it was interesting and warming.

"Perhaps not a lady's drink," he surmised. "However, champagne will have to wait until you are back in England. May I ask why you left?"

"You may. No particularly interesting reason, Captain. My father was going on a thrilling journey, and as the eldest child, I asked to accompany him. Although I had no idea at the time exactly how thrilling it would be."

He nodded and didn't look bored, so she continued.

"Frankly, it seemed a once-in-a-lifetime opportunity. As a woman, I can hardly expect too much excitement to come my way. I'd already had my coming-out Season, and it was fun at first but grew tedious toward the end. I believe I'm not alone in building up my expectations for London's social offerings only to be disappointed."

"Meaning, you fished in the waters of the *bon ton* and didn't capture a rich husband." He cocked his head and eyed her steadily. "For if you had fallen in love in a ballroom, I doubt you would be here in the Orient."

Beryl snapped her mouth closed at his rudeness. Would she be on this ship or the *HMS Wellesley* if she'd fallen in love, eager to join in wedded bliss with Arthur? *No, most definitely not.* Although she had, in fact, caught a rather good fish by all standards.

She didn't particularly want to tell the captain of her triumphant engagement to a viscount. It seemed he would judge her, and she would be diminished in his eyes.

"You're wrong, Captain, If I may say so without sounding vain or ungrateful, I caught a couple fish over the course of the Season, *most* of whom I gladly tossed back."

She liked this analogy, and thinking of the bland kisses she'd shared with a few potential husbands before she'd settled on Lord Wharton, she added, "They went so far as to put their mouths upon my hook hoping I would reel them in."

His eyes widened, but he said nothing. *Was he looking a little shocked?*

"I meant merely a kiss, Captain."

His glance darted to her lips.

Oh dear!

"And they *were* rich fish, by the way," she added. "However, that didn't make them any more desirable."

She sighed. *Poor Arthur.* She ought to, at least, confess to his existence, and while she felt only tepid admiration for him, maybe strong fondness, she still hoped to truly love him some day.

She sipped her drink in the companionable silence with no idea what the man before her was thinking. For her part, she found it hard not to ponder how wonderful it would have been to meet a man during the Season who *did* something with his life, such as the captain.

Undoubtedly, his kiss would have some purpose to it, some dash-fire, not like those she'd experienced from the suitors who simply danced at balls and rode horses in Hyde Park.

Or at least, those men never mentioned doing anything else. Arthur aspired to his father's seat in Parliament and to always keeping good horseflesh, and that was about all.

"I cannot imagine you, Captain, at a ball. Why, I cannot really imagine you—" she broke off.

What was she thinking? She nearly said something inappropriate about dancing and kissing. *And how did her brandy glass become empty anyway?*

To her amazement, he narrowed his eyes at her, leaned forward, slipped his hand behind her head to hold her steady, and kissed her.

"*Mm,*" Beryl murmured as his lips touched hers. A brandy-flavored kiss. *How delightful!*

Then his mouth moved over hers, sending a sensual zing coursing through her. He tilted his head, and their lips seemed to fit together even better.

The sensations she was experiencing were new, unexpected—heady and exhilarating—and she didn't want them to stop.

Her eyes were closed—*when had she closed her eyes?*—but even so, she managed to set her glass down and entwine her fingers behind his neck.

"*Mm,*" she repeated, and this time, he groaned in response.

She seemed to feel his groan as well as hear it. *A very appealing sound!*

Then she felt the tip of his tongue touch her lips, and she gasped, opening her mouth and her eyes at the same time.

She noted his eyes were closed and his dark hair had fallen over his forehead, and then his tongue slipped between her lips and into her mouth, and she closed her eyes again.

When his tongue explored hers, touching, tasting, she got the ludicrous urge to suck it. She did so. The captain groaned again, and she sucked harder.

This was particularly fun, not like any other kiss she'd ever had. And it was a long, drawn-out process, not a quick wet peck as she'd experienced before.

Heavenly!

To her dismay, he lifted his head and drew away.

Opening her eyes, she saw him do the same, languidly, with his gaze a little unfocused. As the captain sat back, releasing her, her hands slid from his shoulders and down his chest, until they broke contact all together.

For a moment, they stared at each other, the captain's dark eyes boring into hers before flickering over her face.

She was certain her cheeks were red, but one main thought occurred and reoccurred.

I would like him to kiss me again.

WHAT THE HELL WAS he thinking? Philip sat back, snatched up his glass, and downed his brandy in a quick gulp. He had better get the hell out of there.

But they continued to look at one another—her eyes curious, even bemused, her mouth looking a little redder than before.

He counted himself damned lucky. Miss Angsley could have shrieked bloody murder. Or slapped him, which she probably should have done.

Yet she seemed to have enjoyed the kiss as much as he had. He wanted to do it again, but then it wouldn't be a spontaneous, forgivable act of impulse when faced with a beautiful woman. Then it would be premeditated and likely to lead to something more. For from her reaction to his kiss, he was fairly confident he could seduce her with little effort.

"Captain?" she asked at his silence.

He shook his head at his own sordid thoughts. He was dead certain she wouldn't want to end up having a tumble in his bed.

More's the pity. Why couldn't he have rescued an experienced woman, a widow or even a strumpet? Why a virginal young lady with her whole life ahead of her, including an aristocratic fish somewhere in London waiting to be caught?

Not that he didn't have a brush with the titled *ton*, himself. His father had been made a baronet by the queen. But Philip was only styled a nobleman by Rufus, who'd nicknamed him Lord Corsair to tease him. Back in England, he would still be plain Philip Carruthers, and certainly no match for Miss Angsley, cousin of an earl.

Standing, he thought to leave, but she rose to her feet as well. To his amazement, she took a step in his direction, her gaze still fixed on his. Then her mouth turned up in the sweetest smile he'd ever seen, and something inside him twitched. It might have been his heart.

Another step closer and her beautiful bosom was a hairsbreadth from his chest. Looking down the front of her new gown, he could easily see the swell of her breasts and past the pretty green bauble on a chain was the deep, mysterious valley between them.

A gentle tug on her bodice, and her nipples would be exposed to his view.

His groin tightened, and he swallowed the lump of desire in his throat.

"Captain." She was staring up at him, her eyes now reminding him of those from a particularly impish horse he'd had as a youth.

"Yes." *Was that his voice, so thick and rough?* He coughed.

"Would you kiss me again?"

Sweet Christ!

"Avast," he said softly, unable to take his eyes off her upturned face.

"I beg your pardon?"

"It means *stop*," he explained. "Because you are too tempting."

She smiled again, and his breath caught at her loveliness. She didn't belong here on the *Robert*. She belonged in a London ballroom, dripping with jewels and finery, surrounded by dandies.

But she *was* here, in his cabin, by some miracle. And she wanted him to kiss her.

He would have to oblige the lady.

With the cabin seeming suddenly hot as Hades, he stripped off the black frock coat he always wore, perfect protection against the wind, handy for a pocket full of spare shot, as well as being some small defense against knife blades.

Tossing it onto the chair, he took her in his arms. With his hands splayed across her back, he drew her the last inch closer so their bodies were pressed together, her warm curves against his chest.

She slid her hands up his cotton shirt and around his neck, and then he felt her fingers entwine in his hair. The small gesture had his loins throbbing.

Lowering his head, he claimed her lips once more. She made the same little humming sound of pleasure, and then he dipped his tongue inside her mouth. Tasting her, stroking her tongue with his, his passions flared, and he had to remind himself again, she was a lady who'd just had her first Season.

Her kiss made him feel, though, as if he were with a skilled Cyprian, one of London's finest, most exclusive whores. Her fingers tugged at his hair as their kiss deepened, and then he felt her hips tilt toward him, as if she were seeking the relief only coupling could provide.

Smoothing his palms down her back and over her shapely bottom, he squeezed her firm flesh. She gasped against his mouth, and he was ready to sweep her onto his bed when suddenly, a shot rang out.

What in blue blazes?

Breaking free from her, he could do little more than send her a regretful glance before racing out of his cabin to see what trouble was afoot.

CHAPTER SEVEN

B efore Philip reached the main deck, he heard another shot. They'd had it too easy, he feared, and the moment he relaxed and tried to enjoy time with a pretty woman, something had to happen.

As it turned out, it was a fairly small something. One of the local fishermen, sounding as though he'd been drinking too much by his shouting and his boasting, had come too close. One of the *Robert*'s night watchmen had warned him away with a pistol fired into the sea. The second time, it had worked.

Philip wished his crew hadn't made anyone aware of their presence, certainly not with the bragging claim he'd heard from one of his men, who'd yelled to the fisherman as he retreated, "That's what you'll get from the *Robert*!"

Better to slip in and out of some harbors anonymously, especially while holding a necklace worth a fortune, though he doubted any of Chui-A-poo's pirates knew his ship by name.

When he turned heel, heading back for his cabin, he suddenly stopped. He was rushing back to Beryl like a rightful lover, when he had absolutely no right to make love to her. She was not his to take. Positively not.

Women of her class had to honor their husband on the wedding night with the gift he wanted to claim right there on his ship.

If he returned to his cabin, he feared he would be overcome by her allure once again. Then, he would ruin her. Though he would make sure she enjoyed it, she wouldn't thank him when it was over.

Knowing he might be insulting her but with no choice, Philip stayed on deck, determined to stay outside until bone tired and then claim a swabbie's bunk again at the other end of the ship.

BERYL WAITED AND WAITED.

Drat!

It was obvious the captain would not return to renew their intimate encounter. She'd thoroughly enjoyed it, only realizing how wrong it was *after* he left and didn't come back.

Kissing a man was better than anything she'd imagined, and when his hands had briefly roamed her body, settling on her bottom—*mercy!*—she could only imagine the delights of the act itself.

Her body had responded without her even thinking about it, getting all hot and prickly, and then curling into him, wanting more.

The *more* would have to wait for her wedding night with Arthur.

Sighing, she had to admit Captain Carruthers knew better by staying away. Without a chaperone or guardian on board, she was the sole protector of her virtue, and with the captain, she'd done a poor job of protecting it.

It was only a kiss, she reminded herself, or two. However, the way her whole body had been humming with excitement, she admitted to herself, she would have given him whatever he wanted to take.

Yes, better he stayed away.

But what would she do with the rest of her evening?

Glancing around, she remembered the brandy bottle, which he'd returned to its hiding place after pouring their drinks. *What other interesting things were in his wardrobe?*

She hoped he didn't mind if she looked. After all, he hadn't said anything was forbidden. Clearly, the chest was, since it was locked, but everything else seemed to be at her disposal.

Unfortunately, there was nothing of interest in the wardrobe, though she did help herself to another sip of his brandy.

Then she spied his coat. In his hurry, he'd left it behind.

Whatever was wrong with her? she wondered, as she sniffed the garment, hoping to commit the scent of him to memory. However, it smelled of the salty sea and something rather mungy and unpleasant.

Perhaps he had a trinket in his pocket, a little jim-jam she could keep to commemorate her first proper kiss, even a coin.

The large outer pockets revealed nothing, but in the breast pocket inside, she found a key.

Smiling to herself, as if playing a game of *hunt the sweet*— a way she amused her younger siblings when home by hiding a boiled sweet and giving them clues—Beryl decided to try out the key in the only lock she'd seen. On the chest.

As it happened, it slid in perfectly, and in an instant, she'd removed the iron lock. On her knees, she opened the trunk lid. There were some papers, which she didn't want to take time to unfold in case she was discovered. There was a hairbrush, which by the look of the captain, would be better in his privy, and some plain cloth, which she realized was covering and protecting delicate blue and white porcelain— a vase, some dishes, even a teapot. Probably all gifts for those back home.

Then she found—*good Lord!*—bags of coins. She could tell what they were by holding one, but peered in each cloth sack anyway to see the gold and silver winking at her. Then she came across a long, wicked-looking knife with an ornate handle such as she'd seen on the junk.

Sitting back on her heels, she frowned. These did appear to be the booty of a pirate. Perhaps he'd even stolen the Chinese porcelain, for that matter. Rather than sweet gifts for his family, maybe this was all pirate plunder.

Her gaze fell upon the pretty, crimson box, which had been with her in the cabin of the Chinese pirate. Recalling how Captain Carruthers had secured it in his bag while looking surprised by her presence, she realized the box was the reason he'd boarded the pirate vessel in the first place.

It wasn't locked, and in a moment, she had it open.

Gasping at the jeweled necklace inside, Beryl felt a moment's panic. A magnificent strand of rubies studded with large, uniform pearls had a ribbon of diamonds interlaced over and under the rubies. More pearls, with a grayish, silvery hue, hung from diamond collets. This was no trinket such as she wore. This was obviously a rare treasure, and worth more than the gold in the sacks, more than the ship she was on, perhaps more than her life.

Captain Carruthers had stolen it from the Chinese pirates who'd stolen it from . . . whom?

She knew one thing. Its rightful owner was not the captain. More likely it belonged to one of the crowned heads of Europe, or even Queen Victoria, herself.

She knew something else. He must truly be a pirate.

Thinking quickly, Beryl removed her own necklace. The chain was gold. The pendant, however, was a common piece of green beryl. Her father had purchased it on the Chinese mainland from a man trying to pass it off as an emerald, which, as she knew from being a curious child with an unusual name, was also included in the beryl gemstone family.

Without hesitation, she put her necklace in the box.

At least if Captain Carruthers picked up the glossy red container, he would assume the jeweled prize was still inside. Then carefully, she put everything back into the trunk, exactly as she'd found it, and set the lock.

Returning the key to the captain's inside pocket, she had another sip from his brandy bottle before setting it in the wardrobe behind his sweaters, then she considered how to hide the necklace. Tonight, she would tie it in her chemise, and tomorrow, she would ask someone for a needle and thread and sew it securely into the hem of her gown. After all, with all the sails on board, there must be a great deal of sewing paraphernalia.

With any luck, Captain Carruthers wouldn't find it missing until many days after she'd sailed away from him.

Her heart still pounding from this rather serious game of hide the sweet, and feeling the strange weight of the necklace pulling down her chemise, Beryl climbed into bed. She lay beside the only witness to her first act of thievery, one orange cat.

THEY LEFT HAIKOU AT first light, and Philip stayed on deck all day, not even going to his cabin for lunch with Miss Angsley. It was for the best. He'd seen neither hide nor hair of her except when a crewman said she'd asked for a needle and thread to sew a tear in her petticoats.

He remembered seeing the garments in a heap in the corner of his cabin. She certainly hadn't been wearing them when he'd felt her body through her silk gown the night before.

Focus, man! he told himself.

All hands were on high alert as they fairly flew across the bay toward Hai Phong. If circumstances went well, they would have about two hours of light to spare when they reached the Kingdom of Việt Nam.

About an hour before their destination, when they passed the single small island in the harbor, the lookout yelled down his report of ships ahead, all congregated at the mouth of the cove, at the head of which was Hai Phong.

"How many?" Philip yelled up to him.

"Four British navy, seven . . . no eight Qing navy. About fifty pirate junks."

Christ! What a mess!

"Engaged in battle, Mr. Reesa?"

"Aye, Captain. Canon balls are flying."

As they got closer, the lookout updated him.

"Seems the battle has been raging a while, Captain. Some junks are already on fire, a Qing ship has capsized."

"How about Her Majesty's ships?"

"Still upright and undamaged, Captain."

Philip had to get a message to the *HMS Wellesley* to call off the battle, if it were over the missing Miss Angsley. Of course, if they were fighting with Shap-ng-tsai, it could as easily be over the sinking of the American ship and three British ships carrying opium the previous autumn. The Royal Navy had already captured a hundred pirate ships, or so rumor had it, up and down the South China Sea, and still, they had yet to find Shap-ng-tsai's main fleet.

This obviously wasn't it either, not unless it had shrunk considerably.

Philip's hunch was as soon as the captain and crew of the *Wellesley* welcomed the diplomat's daughter on board, they would peel away and head home, leaving the battle for the others.

The *Robert* would signal them with the merchant shipping flags on board. Thinking the same thing, Rufus hurried over with the chest of flags and the ship's copy of Captain Marryat's *Code of Signals*. Philip had found it useful on more than one occasion over the past couple of years.

First, he had to get the attention of the British. No better way than cannon fire.

"You there," Philip yelled toward Nick, a swabbie, "go straight to my cabin and tell our guest we are firing our canons. Otherwise, the noise will scare the life out of her."

"Yes, Captain." Nick went off at a run since the order to fire three shots had already been given to the gunner, and the powder monkeys were scrambling.

Sailing to the edge of the battle, the *Robert's* three shots toward the Chinese scattered a few of the junks and got the attention of the Royal Navy as planned.

The first message Rufus spelled out was *daughter*, which was a set code, "2047." The presence of the word in the book of codes had always puzzled Philip in the past, as he couldn't see the reason for having it in the merchant shipping service code book, but now he supposed young ladies were probably getting into trouble all over the globe.

The next group of flags were individual numbers to spell out *Angsley*. That accomplished, the last was a set code for *safe*, "7526."

As his first mate raised the last flag, Philip would swear he heard a cheer from the *Wellesley*, though it must be his imagination.

Instantly, the warship came hard about and left the battle to the other three British ships and the Qing navy.

Philip felt a frisson of regret shiver down his spine. He could have spent last night with Beryl or at least a final meal today. Suddenly, a moment alone became imperative, and he hurried to his cabin, relieving Nick, who had stood sentry at the door.

Then he knocked.

"Come in." Just the sound of her voice, and he felt a rush of pleasure.

Pushing the door open, he found her seated at his table, and his first thought was how he wouldn't mind finding her in his cabin for the rest of his life.

What the hell!

"How are you?" he asked as he closed the door, knowing it to be a rather lame and general question.

Even so, she offered him her sparkling smile.

"I am well. Thank you for sending the warning, or the canon fire would have frightened me."

Nodding, he stood there, feeling a little awkward. They were nearly out of time.

"I've signaled the *Wellesley*, and she is even now on her way to us. I didn't want to sail any closer to the harbor, as there is a skirmish underway. Your father wouldn't thank me for getting you in the line of fire."

"Again, I thank you," she said, standing up. "Also, for lending me your cabin and your books."

She glanced at the bed, upon which Leo had taken up his usual late afternoon position. "And the company of your cat."

All he could do was nod. Philip saw by the shape of her gown, she had put her petticoats back on, looking more like a civilized London lady already. Glancing around the cabin, there was nothing left of her there. When she disembarked his ship, it would be as if she'd never graced the *Robert* with her presence.

He wanted to slap himself for getting sentimental over a woman he'd only known for a few days, but he couldn't deny the unwelcome pangs he was feeling.

After their extraordinary kiss, he wondered if she felt the same.

Watching her walk toward a porthole, he knew the moment she saw her father's ship. She gasped.

"It's nearly upon us. Oh," she exclaimed excitedly. "I can see my father on deck!"

Turning to him, her eyes were dancing.

"Let's get you reunited, then," he said, knowing he sounded stiff.

"It seems as if I've been here a long time," she added, leaning over to stroke Leo. To his amazement, she bent low and kissed the top of the cat's head.

When next she looked at Philip, he could see tears in her eyes.

She waved her hands futilely in front of her face.

"My apologies, Captain. I'm feeling emotional."

"It's understandable. You've been through quite an adventure. It's been my pleasure to play a part."

The tide of tears stemmed, she shot him a smile. "You didn't seem to be always too happy about it," she pointed out, making him smile in return.

"I was a little gruff, I admit."

She approached him, and his mouth went dry.

"Understandable," she echoed his word. "I was not in your plans when you boarded the pirate junk."

"No," he agreed, "not in my plans."

She was directly in front of him now, when he heard the boatswain's whistle signaling the arrival of the *Wellesley*. It was his last chance to kiss her again. Mesmerized by her eyes and her lips, he couldn't pass it up.

Keeping his hands to himself, he leaned close, watching her shut her eyes, and then he brushed his lips across hers.

Utterly unsatisfying! He needed to hold her tightly, pull her against him—

The knock on his cabin door drove them apart.

"Lord Corsair, the Royal Navy has arrived." It was Rufus's mocking voice.

"Coming," he called out, staring down into Beryl's face, memorizing it.

She tilted her head, looking achingly beautiful.

Would he ever again meet a woman who sparked in him such yearning?

"I shall be sure to tell my father what great care you took of me."

That was reassuring. Elsewise, the assumption might be he'd taken advantage and kissed her, exactly as he had, or worse, ravished her, precisely as he wanted to do.

Opening the door and stepping aside, he gestured for her to proceed him, snagging his frock coat from the chair where he'd left it the day before. He wanted to look his best for meeting Lord Angsley, lest the man think him a scruffy pirate.

CHAPTER EIGHT

Less than an hour later, Beryl was on the *Wellesley* heading home. It would take a third of a year, maybe a little more. At that moment, though, her thoughts were with a particular man on another ship, its whereabouts unknown to her.

What had the other man called him? Lord Corsair?

She wished she'd had the chance to ask the captain why. Instead, within moments, she was on deck, surrounded by the *Robert*'s crew and then by her father and his contingent.

Her father had been beyond grateful, thanking Captain Carruthers, pumping his hand up and down and slapping him on the back. The captain had looked bemused, even more so when Lord Angsley said he would write a letter of gratitude to Queen Victoria and ask her to publicly commend him and the entire crew of the *Robert*.

"Much appreciated, my lord," Captain Carruthers had quipped, then ruining the solemn moment, he'd added, "but coin of the realm would be preferable over commendation."

Ha! She'd nearly laughed out loud. He'd proven himself again to be a pirate who wanted only gold and jewels. Her father faltered a moment, appearing taken aback.

"I'm speaking only in jest, my lord," the captain amended. "Of course, there is no price which could be put upon the safe return of your daughter. While I am not in the Royal Navy, still, I was happy to do service to queen and country."

Beryl rolled her eyes. He made it sound as if he'd gone searching for her rather than happening upon her while stealing a jeweled necklace, even one already stolen.

And then it was over, and she barely got to say goodbye. First, she offered a general thank you to the crew who were standing around listening, and then, she let Captain Carruthers take her hand and bow over it.

Very much a gentleman.

How she wished they'd had time for a deeper, final kiss in his cabin, one she could cherish. She'd been waiting since he'd left her the evening before. Instead, she had barely felt the whisper of his lips across hers.

That evening, in her own lovely stateroom on the *Wellesley*, reunited with her maid and all her belongings, Beryl considered unpicking the sewn hem of her gown and withdrawing the necklace from its hiding place. Then she thought better of it. She wouldn't wear the gown again on the voyage home. She would put it away and the necklace with it.

Hesitating before dropping the pale green silk into the bottom of her trunk, she wondered if she should show her father the jewels immediately. In her heart, however, she believed it would cause him to think badly of her rescuer—to consider him the *pirate* Captain Carruthers—while, at present, her father was full of praise and gratitude.

No. When she was once more in London, she would decide what to do, perhaps asking her best friend, Eleanor Blackwood, who had a good head on her shoulders. After all, Beryl could not simply appear at Buckingham Palace, request an audience with Queen Victoria, and then inquire as to whether the queen had lost any of her jewels.

PHILIP WAS SORRY TO see Miss Angsley go. He couldn't deny it. He also knew he'd better get himself into the next friendly port and find a willing woman to tup.

However, even while watching the wake of the *Wellesley* as it sailed for the Riau Archipelago, his lookout announced they were under attack.

"Sails, ahoy!"

It took Philip but an instant to regain his concentration and discover the danger wasn't coming from the harbor and Shap-ng-tsai's ships off their starboard but from their port side. A small fleet of junks were coming upon them from the east, perhaps having waited for the British warship to leave.

"Christ!" Philip exclaimed. "All hands!"

The boatswain blew his whistle, calling all hands to their stations.

Obviously, Chui-A-poo wasn't going to let the necklace go easily, after all. And here they were, temporarily dead in the water. That, however, was the beauty of a three-masted clipper.

"Haul the wind," he ordered his crew.

Though primarily a peaceful mission, they'd had their share of encounters, and every crewman of the *Robert* had either been a merchant seaman or a navy man. In the shake of a lamb's tail, sailors were manning the lines and gunners were at the cannons, ready for battle.

Philip didn't like their odds at close quarters, not with only a dozen junks.

"Hard about," he called to Rufus at the helm. "We need the Royal Navy."

Thus, instead of sailing to a friendly port and enjoying shore leave, Philip found himself sailing directly toward the skirmish in the Hai Phong harbor. While there were still three British ships to help him, going into the midst of another battle seemed the best option.

To his relief, the other pirates didn't follow but stayed close to the small island of Dao Bach, the only land for miles in any direction.

His relief died after the first few hours and was buried at the bottom of the sea when they ended up fighting for three days alongside the Royal Navy and the Qing navy. Afterward, he learned they'd helped destroy fifty-eight pirate junks carrying twelve hundred cannons and three thousand pirates.

Six junks escaped, as did Shap-ng-tsai, but since he hadn't been the pirate to take Miss Angsley, it didn't matter. The blow to his fleet had sent him fleeing farther west, and Philip couldn't imagine the pirate regaining control over the coastal villages he'd terrorized before.

Moreover, in the interim, sometime in the middle of the second night during the lull in battle, Chui-A-poo's handful of junks had vanished. Philip could only hope they'd headed back to China. Maybe they didn't want to wait until the British were free to turn their attention on them. Or maybe they'd assumed the *Robert* was going that way, too, after the battle of Hai Phong. They were wrong.

Taking the same tack as the *Wellesley*, Philip ordered their course for the Java Sea—and home—anchoring that evening at the southern point of Dat Mui in the Gulf of Siam. For a few hours, all was quiet.

In the pitch black, they were set upon.

Like a dragon, Chui-A-poo sent flaming balls of gunpowder onto the *Robert*'s decks. While the lookout screamed the danger, and the *Robert*'s bleary-eyed crew scrambled to put out the fires, Chui-A-poo's pirates climbed aboard from row boats below, using the cover of the first attack to hide their grappling hooks.

Philip shot more than one before he was overcome and dragged into his own cabin by two pirates while their leader and another guard walked calmly behind.

Ordered to light his lamps, Philip did so and faced Chui-A-poo.

"Where is she?" the pirate asked, gesturing for his guard to check behind the small door to the privy.

She! They were here for Beryl?

"You speak English," Philip stalled.

"Obviously," Chui-A-poo said. "Do you? I asked you a question."

There was only one answer, and they would know it anyway, after they searched his ship.

"She was taken by one of the British ships." He thought he'd phrased that well, putting the blame elsewhere.

Chui clenched his hands and closed his eyes. When he opened them, he punched Philip directly in the face, snapping his head back.

"She was a rare jewel. Even named after one. Only an idiot would let her get away. Like my captain, who I killed for his stupidity in losing the girl to you."

Feeling blood trickling from where his teeth had cut his mouth and cheek, Philip could only hope he wouldn't be the next to perish for the same crime—while fairly confident he would be.

He was going to die over rescuing Beryl.

Considering the thought, he supposed it was an upstanding, honorable reason to perish. He wished he'd got to tup her first, but that was rather selfish of him.

Chui-A-poo gave his guard orders, probably to search the rest of the *Robert* for Beryl. The man quickly departed. Philip liked his odds better and wondered if he stalled long enough, perhaps Rufus would rescue him.

"She was kidnapped for you?" he asked the pirate leader.

Chui didn't bother to answer. Instead, he said, "She would have been an honored and cherished wife."

Wife? There was that Chinese pirate code again. Marry the pretty ones, give back the plain ones, and don't rape any of them unless you wanted your head cut off and thrown into the sea, which had saved Beryl from that fate.

If the kidnapped girl had been for Chui, then maybe he didn't know of the—

"Where is the necklace?" the pirate demanded.

The devil! Both jewels—Beryl and the necklace—belonged to Chui-A-poo.

"I had *two* treasures," Chui-A-poo added. "I had better still have one."

"Yes," Philip muttered, thinking of the failure of his two-year mission. If he hadn't waited to reunite father and daughter, he would have been rounding the Cape of Good Horn in a few weeks. Instead, he was likely to be slaughtered where he stood.

On the other hand, perhaps he could give the duchess's necklace back and live to tell the tale. If he and the crew survived, they could always hunt it down again.

"Release me," he demanded. He could hardly do the pirate leader's bidding with his arms held.

Chui-A-poo nodded to his men. When Philip's arms were free, he wiped the blood from his face with the back of his hand.

"If I return the necklace to you, you will let my crew and my ship go free."

Chui raised an eyebrow. "What about your own life? Are you offering to sacrifice it for your crew?"

Philip decided to be honest. "I had assumed I would go *with* my ship and crew."

To his amazement, Chui-A-poo laughed. When he stopped, though, Philip saw no mirth at all in the pirate's black eyes.

"Will you beg?" the pirate leader asked.

"No," Philip answered at once. *Dammit!* He was a Carruthers, raised on the same stretch of coast as the famed pirate Avery who claimed to have buried three chests full of glorious treasure in the sands of the Cornish shore, and he wouldn't tarnish the legacy of the fearless men of Cornwall.

Besides, death meant seeing Robert again, and he intended to give his twin a good thrashing for dying so stupidly in a carriage accident. If he hadn't, Philip had no doubt he never would have undertaken this fool's venture.

Chui-A-poo looked at him and grunted. Then he shrugged.

"Give me the necklace."

They didn't exactly have any kind of spoken bargain, but the power was all in the pirate's hands. At least Philip did have the necklace. If not, his death would have been immediate. Reaching into his coat, he pulled out the key to the lock.

"If I may," he said, gesturing to the other side of the cabin.

Chui nodded and the two pirates let Philip pass, and then he knelt by the chest, opened the lock, and after a moment, retrieved the red-lacquered box.

Should he toss the small container at the far wall of the cabin and try to escape?

Most likely, he would feel a blade of steel in his back before he took a step.

"How did you come upon the necklace?" Philip asked, returning to stand before the pirate leader.

Chui eyed him. "On my orders, it was stolen from a Qing official who stole it from a servant to the Imperial Palace." He smiled and added, "Who stole it from the emperor's emissary to Britain, who—"

"Who stole it from Buckingham Palace," Philip finished.

"No," Chui said. "Who stole it from the emissary's servant who stole it from Buckingham Palace."

Then he laughed heartily, probably at the notion he, the pirate leader of a grand fleet of pirates, had managed to get something that the emperor and the government of the Manchus couldn't hold onto.

Watching as Chui set Philip's confiscated pepperbox revolver on the table, his glance took in his candlestick, too. Beryl apparently had rummaged in his wardrobe, found its hiding place, and set it back on the table, perhaps as a jest.

Chui held his hands out, and Philip placed the box in them, watching as he opened the container.

From his angle, Philip could see a sparkle of gold and green. *Green?*

"What is this?" Chui-A-poo bellowed, reaching in and pulling out Beryl's necklace.

What, indeed! Philip wanted to roar, as well. In the space of a heartbeat, he knew what had happened. *She'd stolen his booty! And now he would die.*

The other two pirates leaned forward to get a look at what the box contained.

And then Philip's luck changed. Leo, undetected under the table, yowled like a devilish fiend. One of the others must have trod upon his tail.

Everyone jumped at the hair-raising sound, and all three pirates looked down, searching for the unholy creature.

It was as good a diversion as any. Thrusting his hand forward, Philip snatched his gun with one hand and, for good measure, the candlestick with the other before darting backward.

They were at extremely close range, but there was no choice. Philip shot the first of the pirates who moved, and then heard the terrible sound of the empty revolver chamber as he tried to shoot the second one. He had fired his last ball.

Before the other pirate could understand his good fortune, Philip whacked him in the face with the candlestick's base. As the man grabbed his bashed nose, Philip struck him hard on the head. He dropped like a stone.

Beryl was right. It was a decent weapon. However, seeing how she'd stolen his necklace, nearly getting him killed in the process, he didn't like her as much as he had before.

Ready to fight one-on-one with Chui-A-poo, candlestick to sword, Philip turned only to find the pirate leader had vanished.

Reaching over, he abandoned the brass candlestick and opened the tin cannister on his table. Grabbing a hand full of .42-inch lead balls, he dropped some into his pocket and then reloaded his gun, filling each of the six chambers.

Chasing after the pirate leader, Philip had a feeling this wasn't over yet. On deck, things were looking grim. Most of his crew sat in a circle, Chinese pirates guarding them. Two of his men lay either dead or wounded. No sign of Rufus, which worried him.

For the second time that night, Philip had to kill without choice. He started shooting any pirate who moved. Those who didn't fall to the deck scrambled over the side, splashing into the water below. Chui-A-poo was nowhere to be seen and had probably already fled back to his own junk. The man would live to fight another day.

That was what worried Philip most.

And where the hell was Rufus?

Unfortunately, his answer came when he found the pirate leader's guard, who'd been searching the *Robert* as ordered. He and Rufus had obviously fought and now the guard lay face down and Rufus was bleeding profusely.

Opening his eyes when Philip approached, Rufus ground out, "I'm not dead yet. Can't say the same for this one, though." He nudged the pirate with the toe of his boot.

"Lot of blood, my friend," Philip told his first mate.

"My arm mostly," Rufus reported. "Bastard got a good couple slices in before I killed him. Take more than that, though. Remember I'm related to John Gow—"

"I know, I've heard it before." Philip hoped he wouldn't continue.

"A notorious pirate who became captain of the *Revenge*, God rest his soul," Rufus continued as if Philip hadn't spoken.

He'd heard the story before as Rufus somewhat dubiously trailed his lineage back to an ill-fated red-haired buccaneer.

Now wasn't the time, however, for an adventure story. They were having one of their own, and Philip was ready to end it.

"My father is a famed wool merchant," Philip added, "and he won't help us anymore than your old dead pirate relation who, may I remind you, was hanged not once but twice. Poor unfortunate bastard!"

Rufus had told the tale many times of how John Gow's friends, trying to help him to die swiftly, yanked on his feet. When the rope broke with the pirate still alive, he'd had to be hanged again.

"Curses to those who used a thin rope the first time," Rufus declared.

Philip dropped to his knees to assess the damage before helping his first mate to stand. Rufus wavered slightly, grasping hold of his captain's arm with his good hand.

"Christ almighty! We need to get you bandaged and sewn."

Leaning Rufus against the hull, Philip bent down and tore off the dead pirate's shirt, then quickly tied it around his first mate's upper arm.

"I can't have you bleeding all over the ship."

In silence, they made their way back on deck to view the damage. Their sails had been furled for the night, so were largely undamaged except for a burned topsail and a singed lower course. More worrisome was the smoldering decking, which the carpenter was already inspecting.

In the daylight, the crew would have to hang on ropes to examine the *Robert*'s sides, making sure they were still seaworthy. Repairs would further delay their return trip, making the passage round the cape even more dangerous. Not to mention the present peril of remaining anchored off Việt Nam. They would have to sail slowly north into the Gulf of Siam for better protection.

Meanwhile, after quickly disposing of the pirates' bodies, they wrapped their own two dead crewmen in the singed flax canvas sails and, after Philip performed a solemn service, sent them to Davy Jones's locker. It didn't sit well with him. No necklace, regardless how beautiful or dripping with jewels, was worth the price they'd paid that night.

Moreover, Beryl was to blame for all his bad luck.

Later, over cups of rum in his first mate's quarters—a bunk against the wall with a half wall separating it from the rest of the crew's bunks—Philip told Rufus of their guest's unbelievable trickery of switching the necklaces.

"The wench had more gumption than I gave her credit for," Rufus said, looking pale and lying down but drinking rum all the same. "Not a terrible thing, either, her stealing our treasure. Elsewise, the duchess's necklace would be heading back to Bias Bay by now."

Rufus was right about that, but Philip wasn't willing to give her any credit for her deception. It had nearly cost him his life.

"Let's drink to Leo, for without him, I'd be dead, the ship would've been taken, and you probably would've bled out on the deck," he reminded his first mate.

They toasted his dead brother's cat.

Then Philip made a silent vow. He would hunt down Beryl Angsley, retrieve his necklace so he could claim his reward, and he would demand reparation for his dead crewmembers' families to boot.

CHAPTER NINE

London, England

"Please come," Beryl wrote to Eleanor Blackwood. "Eleven o'clock at our townhouse on Wednesday."

She'd only been back in London for a few days, but the necklace's presence in her bedroom weighed heavily on her. Over tea, she would discuss it with Eleanor.

Luckily, her father had so much business in Town, he had no intention of dragging his daughter back to their country estate. Instead, her mother and siblings had all come to London for the happy reunion.

She hadn't even seen her fiancé yet and wondered at her own lack of pressing need to do so. Instead, she'd written Arthur a letter, telling him of her return. Perhaps he was no longer in London or had given up on their engagement sometime during the course of her travels.

Why did that possibility cause her absolutely no concern at all?

As for her family, the Angsleys had quickly grown used to the return of father and daughter into their midst. Her mother was happy to go on the social rounds, taking Beryl with her, and her young siblings were delighted to bicker and torment her as usual. It was heaven. She didn't think she would ever want to leave Britain again.

Maybe for a tour of the continent, but she had no desire for another long sea voyage or any possible encounter with pirates.

No matter how handsome.

And kissable.

She sighed, feeling restless whenever she thought of Captain Caruthers—or *Lord Corsair*, as she recalled his first mate calling him before she left his cabin for the last time. In truth, he wasn't really a lord of the realm at all, not a peer. Simply the son of a baronet, and not even a hereditary title at that.

But he had dash-fire to spare.

Beryl decided against mentioning to her father that the captain was the twin brother of the man who'd nearly killed their family member, John Angsley, her father's only nephew and Beryl's beloved cousin. She didn't think it would make a difference, and she saw no reason to bring up the tragic matter. In any case, keeping his word, her father penned a letter to the queen recounting the tale Beryl had told him of her rescue.

Of course, she didn't mention the captain's wonderful kisses or how her heart thumped and her body warmed whenever he was close to her.

She sighed again. In a week, she was going to her first ball in a year. She wrote to Arthur telling him of her intent and, within hours, received a return missive. He would meet her there for their grand reunion. She could only hope he had developed some of the magnetism of Philip Carruthers.

THE ENTIRE VOYAGE BACK to the British Isles, the *Robert* raced like the devil himself was in their wake. And for all Philip knew, he was. No one had ever seen a Chinese pirate fleet outside of the Indian Ocean, but it didn't mean Chui-A-poo wasn't going to come after the necklace that had slipped through his fingers.

Unlikely, though.

And it had slipped through Philip's fingers, too. But at least he knew the minx who had it.

As they sailed into the English Channel, he gave a nod and a small salute to the Cornish coastline. For if Rufus were obsessively proud of his pirate ancestor, Philip, whose Carruthers lineage was also Scottish a few generations prior, was equally proud of his mother's people, Cornish through and through.

Then they passed Plymouth, where Beryl's Royal Naval ship would have docked in the heart of the navy's stronghold. The *Wellesley* couldn't have been far ahead of the *Robert*. Even after delaying for repairs, they'd run at nearly eighteen knots for much of the voyage, where the warship couldn't have done more than eight. Then she and her father and the other diplomats would have travelled over land to London.

And that's where Philip would find her. Beryl had asked him if he were actually a pirate. If he was, then he wasn't a particularly good one. He could only imagine the disdain of Rufus's favorite pirate, John Gow, at Philip being bested by a slip of an English lass.

Tricked out of his own treasure!

When the *Robert* finally sailed up the Thames to St. Katharine Docks, his men cheered their return home despite the increasing aroma emanating from the brown river as they approached London.

Philip burned to jump ship and race into the fancy section of London where the Angsleys undoubtedly had a townhouse, probably in Mayfair. Ready to beat down her door and demand his stolen prize, he counseled himself to have patience, to bide his time.

First, he had to greet his own family, then he had to contact the families of the deceased, and then he had to make a report to his queen.

"Your humble servant has discharged his duty and found the necklace. And lost the necklace, Your Majesty. However, it is here on English soil. I merely have to find it."

Yes, that would go over well.

He decided he would wait on the report until he had the duchess's jewelry back in hand. Besides, without it, he wouldn't receive the bounty and thus could not pay his men. Many of his crew would come back to the ship daily until their promised wages were delivered.

His parents were glad to see he'd survived. That was the extent of it. It seemed after Robert's untimely and shocking demise, they'd decided to protect their own hearts by lavishing their love upon the two younger children who had no resemblance—and thus, no reminder—to their lost son.

Though twins, Robert was the first born, and all praise and hopes and dreams had been placed squarely on his shoulders. Especially after Philip took twice as long to learn to read, then set fire to his grammar school and got into fisticuffs at St. Paul's boarding school on more than one occasion.

His parents had practically considered him a black sheep. Not a pleasant pronouncement from a family making their living from the finest wool. The offensive black wool, not being dyable, was worth less, and Philip had always felt himself to be the less worthy son.

Nevertheless, he had loved his twin, who'd never said a bad word about his shenanigans. In Robert's absence, his younger brother and sister were absolutely delighted to see their brother's return, more than making up for his parents' coolness.

After distributing presents all around—tea, porcelain, silk, jade hair combs, and plum wine—the next day he visited with the families of the deceased. Recalling how he felt when the news of Robert's death reached him, he could only offer his own futile condolences, sincerely thank the families for giving him their menfolk, and assure them compensation would be forthcoming.

And then he was free to find Miss Angsley.

NOT A DROP OF dash-fire to be found, Beryl thought after ten minutes at the ball. Every man seemed pallid and dull, utterly uninteresting compared to—

She stopped herself. This simply wouldn't do. She couldn't start comparing ordinary London gentlemen to Captain Carruthers. If she did, she would find herself alone and unengaged.

Speaking of which, as if the ton knew this was their first meeting in nearly a year, people were stepping back, making way as Lord Arthur Wharton approached her.

Dear Arthur. Of a decent height so she didn't have to crane her neck too high, with sandy brown hair and kind eyes, he approached her, a decidedly bland smile on his ordinary face.

Had he always been so pale, reminding her of blancmange, a dessert she detested?

Taking her hand, he bent over it, though not kissing her gloved knuckles.

"You have returned," he said in his normal, calm voice, as if they'd only just seen each other a week earlier.

Beryl sighed at the passionless words from her husband-to-be, for whom she felt no more than for any of the other men in the room.

Drat!

Where was the frisson of excitement? Somewhere back on the high seas with Philip Carruthers—that was the truthful, albeit unhappy, answer.

It would simply take time for her to recall how much she cared for her viscount. The comparison with a ship's captain and a rakish pirate to boot was unfair.

"You look well," he continued, releasing her hand.

"As do you, my lord. It is good to see you." She swallowed the lump in her throat, which indicated she was lying through her teeth.

"It must seem strange to be back in Britain and surrounded by your family and friends. I imagine you were lonely on your voyage."

Actually, as the only female on board a naval vessel, she'd had to fight for a minute alone. However, every single moment with any of Her Majesty's officers had also been spent with her father or maid as chaperone. In any case, although some were handsome or clever, they were all a little too upstanding.

Rather like Arthur. *If they were alone at that moment, would he draw her to him and kiss her, would he tell her how much he'd longed her?*

For, truly, not a single man who'd paid her any mind on board the *Wellesley* seemed the type who would grab her close and kiss her fiercely. Neither did her fiancé.

Of course, there was more to life than being kissed. And she certainly wanted to experience all of what followed a kiss.

So why was she having trouble picturing anyone except Captain Carruthers?

"What are you thinking?" Eleanor asked her, as they waited for the next waltz. "You have a moonish expression."

"*Moonish?* Is that even a word?"

Eleanor laughed. "If not, it should be."

With Eleanor's next dance partner and Arthur chatting close by, Beryl's best friend lowered her voice and whispered in her ear, "Contemplating Lord Corsair?"

Beryl almost wished she hadn't told Eleanor everything, but that's what best friends did. Unfortunately, they still hadn't decided how to handle the issue of the necklace.

Eleanor's suggestion, while prudent, seemed extremely time-consuming—to go to the offices of the *London Times* and read every issue printed in the past three years to find any mention of the theft of such an extraordinary piece of jewelry.

Her friend's second suggestion was simply to give it to Beryl's father and let him deal with it. Beryl had a feeling he would be angry to learn she'd kept it from him in the first place. Thus, since it didn't seem to matter to anyone, she did nothing, biding her time.

One week slipped into the next, as one dance drifted into another, sometimes with her fiancé, sometimes with another partner.

At the next ball, Beryl stood momentarily by herself with Arthur somewhere in the room bending the ear of a member of parliament and her mother seated close, as always. Eleanor had only just deserted her side for the ladies retiring room, and Beryl was staring down at her saffron-colored gown.

With a start, it dawned on her it was the same color as Leo's fur. She hoped the cat and his owner were faring well.

Not paying any attention to who reached for her dance card and scratched his name upon it, all at once, she heard *his* voice.

"Miss Angsley, I have penciled myself in for the next dance."

Snapping her gaze up, she couldn't help gasping, standing there like a gaping fish as Captain Carruthers released her dance card, letting it swing upon her wrist.

"Captain!" She thought of two things at once, his kisses and the necklace. Her hand fluttered up to the golden-yellow beryl pendant she wore that evening, as if the purloined jewels would suddenly appear around her neck.

Was he extraordinarily angry with her?

His glance followed the movement of her hand to her throat, and then returned to her eyes, undoubtedly guessing her thoughts.

"At your service, Miss Angsley."

If he was at her service, why did his tone sound annoyed, even tight and unfriendly? She knew exactly why—he wanted his stolen jewels.

And all she wanted was to throw her arms around him.

"How can you be *here?*" she asked, feeling slow-witted. *Wasn't he on the* Robert *sailing upon some ocean somewhere?*

"London is my home. True, this ball is beyond tedious, and I can think of places I would rather be." While he spoke, he took up her hand and bowed over it, even going so far as to bring her gloved knuckles to his lips.

Sadly, she felt it to be entirely for show and without any true feeling.

Then he added, "However, I sought you out and was told you were here. Thus, here I am."

Again, she gasped. *He sought her out!*

"You came to the ball seeking *my* company?"

As soon as she asked, she realized the absurdity of both her question and the emotions swirling within her head and heart. Obviously, he was there for the necklace, and that alone, and soon, he would bring it up.

His dark eyes narrowed. "We have time before our dance. Would you care for some lemonade or champagne?"

The captain was offering her a beverage at a ball in London. *How utterly surreal!*

Taking his measure, Beryl realized his hair was combed and trimmed, and his clothes were entirely fashionable.

Why did she feel a slight disappointment?

Did this real-life Philip Carruthers match the one in her memory? *What if she'd imagined everything? The spark? The excitement of his kiss?*

She'd held close the thrilling notion he would have done more with her—and *to* her—if not for the interruption during their second kiss when he'd been called on deck.

However, that was *before* he'd discovered her duplicity. She supposed it changed everything.

"Champagne, if you please," she said, knowing she was still staring at him as if he were a zoo animal.

With her request, he disappeared into the throng.

Glancing around, she spied her mother's rich sapphire-blue gown. Miss Angsley was deep in conversation with another mother. So, she hadn't seen the captain.

And where was Eleanor? Beryl wanted someone to attest to the sighting of him, to tell her she wasn't losing her sanity.

Thankfully, her best friend reappeared.

"They had French perfume in the retiring room. Smell," Eleanor said, leaning in close so Beryl could sniff her neck.

"Heavenly. Listen, you'll never believe it, but Captain Carruthers is here."

"What!" Eleanor exclaimed loudly. "Where? Point him out this instant or I shall die of curiosity."

For the first time since seeing the captain, Beryl relaxed with a laugh. Her friend was the same old Eleanor, enthusiastic and giddy. What's more, she, herself, was safe in London. The general air of menace that lingered throughout her voyage had no power over her here. Thus, there was no reason to get worked up or to be anxious by the captain's appearance.

Except for the fact she'd taken something of great value from him, and he wanted it back.

"He has gone to fetch me some champagne," Beryl told Eleanor, who grinned.

"*He* has returned with your champagne," Philip's voice stated clearly behind them.

Beryl, along with Eleanor, turned slowly to face him. She felt her friend give a small start. After all, Philip Carruthers was divinely handsome, and he had come all the way from China to the Mallory's ball to see her! Despite knowing he'd done so for the necklace, it still tickled her to have him cross the globe and attend a ball to get close to her.

What's more, he had not one but two glasses of champagne, which he now held out to them.

"How did you . . . ?" began Eleanor.

"I saw from across the room Miss Angsley had company," he said, addressing Eleanor. "I would never leave a lady parched."

Doubtful, thought Beryl. The extra champagne was probably for him. However, it was a nice gesture.

"Captain Carruthers, this is my dearest friend, Miss Blackwood."

The captain took Eleanor's free, gloved hand in his and nodded over it without kissing it. Beryl was watching intently, comparing the greeting he'd given her to that which he gave Eleanor.

She shook her head at her own ridiculousness. *She wasn't really going to feel a twinge of jealousy a mere few minutes after seeing the man, was she?* After all, her fiancé was somewhere about, and she'd been held by various men at dances since her return to London. Whereas, she and Eleanor might be the first women the captain had touched since his journey.

Foolishly, she hoped that was the case.

"When did you arrive home, Captain?" she asked to clarify.

"Only two days hence."

"And here you are," Eleanor observed, darting Beryl a look, "already out and about at a ball. Do you like to dance so very much?"

Beryl heard the mirth in her friend's voice. Obviously, Eleanor was urging him to admit what he liked so very much was, in fact, Beryl. She and Eleanor had discussed the kisses from every aspect and angle. Moreover, Eleanor, a romantic who had yet to experience a true love of her own, was convinced the captain had fallen madly for her friend.

Had Eleanor not considered how Beryl's pilfering of the captain's booty might have changed any warm feelings he'd had? Beryl was positive he had only the sparkling jewels on his mind that night.

The captain paused a moment, glanced over their heads at the ballroom, and then back at Eleanor.

"Miss Blackwood, I am not so keen a dancer in truth, especially after the time spent away from this type of affair, only to return and find it exactly unchanged."

"I see," Eleanor said. "While you have changed from your travels, London has not. Yet perhaps it didn't need to. Perhaps the social aspect of London is precisely as it should be for the people who enjoy it."

The captain offered his first small smile of the evening. "You are wise beyond your years, Miss Blackwood."

Eleanor blushed prettily. "It is only that I agree up to a point. I, for one, find the Season and its events to be a necessary evil, though I prefer to be at my family's country home."

Beryl thought she might be witnessing the beginning of a *tendre*, half expecting the captain to agree on the merits of the country and whisk Eleanor away to a happy life among flowers and birds.

She was being small-minded and, again, feeling the green haze of jealousy—so utterly unlike her. She'd never given a thought as to whether Arthur was keeping company with anyone else during her long time away.

"Since you wrote your name on my card," Beryl interjected, "and our waltz is about to begin, may I inquire whether you wish to dance?"

"In fact, I do," he said, taking the glass from her hands and putting it on a nearby table. "If you will excuse us, Miss Blackwood."

After nodding to Eleanor, he led her onto the parquet floor.

"Balls are tedious, and you don't particularly like to dance," Beryl reminded him as they began to move in the formation of other dancers. "So why are we?"

"Dancing together, especially the waltz with no changing of partners, is a perfect way to speak privately without drawing attention."

She'd been correct. "I see."

"Let us make use of our very limited time, shall we? You stole something from me, and I want it back."

CHAPTER TEN

Beryl had been ready for this declaration since the moment she'd seen him. Of course he wanted it back! He was a pirate.

"Is it yours?"

His wolfish grin made something inside her stomach twist uncomfortably. She wanted to touch his face, stroke her fingers through his hair when he smiled like that.

"Impertinent question," Philip said, "from someone who broke into someone else's trunk and stole what doesn't belong to her."

She raised an eyebrow. "I imagine it has been stolen before."

"A few times over, in fact," he agreed.

"Then how is my relieving you of its possession any different than the previous thieveries which brought the item onto your ship and into your trunk? How is it any different from your own pilfering?"

She felt him sigh with his whole body.

"I still cannot believe you took the key from my coat and helped yourself to a good snooping around in my personal belongings, especially after I rescued you and gave you the hospitality of my own cabin."

It sounded terrible when he said it that way. Except . . .

"I fail to see how the *item* is your personal belonging. Besides, with your coloring, it wouldn't suit you in the least." She spoke in jest but felt like stomping on his foot.

At her words, the captain seemed to see her for the first time, staring into her eyes a moment before starting to laugh.

"That was humorous," he said finally. Then a moment later, his demeanor grew serious again. "I trusted you."

She grimaced. *Why did his statement, set in the past, bother her? Who cared if a pirate trusted her or not?*

"You will return the necklace to me," he insisted.

"Because it will fetch you a great deal of money," she guessed.

"Of course. Because it was my mission, a charge from the queen."

"Pish!" she told him.

"Again, *pish?* How dare you?"

She shrugged while dancing, knowing it was decidedly unladylike.

"I dare because you could say anything and expect me to believe it."

He looked nearly apoplectic, as if he wanted to strangle her, and even looked handsome while doing so.

"Yes, I sailed all the way to the Orient to recover the necklace," he ground out. Then, with a scoffing tone, he added, "Unfortunately, I recovered you, as well."

Oh! Now he was simply being mean.

"Then I shall return it to her myself," Beryl told him, pleased to see his look of displeasure.

"You will not. It is not your place to—"

"Thank you for the dance, Captain," Beryl said, as the music ended. "Despite your not liking to do so, you are an excellent partner."

Before he could say anything more, she turned and walked away. Hopefully, Arthur was close, perhaps looking for her. If not, she would disappear into the throng, for she had a feeling Philip Carruthers wouldn't be dismissed so easily.

JAW CLENCHED, PHILIP WATCHED Beryl walk away with a confident sway of her hips. His annoyance battled with his attraction for her. As soon as he'd seen her across Lord Mallory's spacious ballroom, he'd felt the pull of desire as strongly as upon his ship.

However, she was being unnecessarily difficult, and he couldn't allow it to continue. He had men and their families to pay.

Thus, he followed her until she settled next to a gentleman who'd been engaged in conversation with someone else but who focused on her as soon as she appeared.

Who wouldn't? In her stunning orange-yellow gown, undoubtedly silk brought back from the Orient, Beryl was exotically beautiful.

Then their hands briefly touched, Beryl's and this stranger's. She leaned close and said something. The man smiled, tucked her hand under his arm, and led her away.

Philip hated him instantly. However, he wasn't going to cause a scene, and it was obvious she was not going to cooperate, not when it was so easy to walk away.

Thus, a few hours later, acting the very pirate she believed him to be, he found entrance into her family's townhouse off Hanover Square, via the back alley and a particularly sturdy trellis.

Leaving Leo at the bottom—the stubborn animal still accompanied him uninvited on anything smacking of adventure, by jumping into a carriage or on top of it if denied entrance—Philip began to climb.

Even with the thorny roses, the ascent was nothing compared to climbing a mast to reach the skysail. He supposed he could have picked the lock of the servants' entrance to the basement, but then he would have to risk being caught going up at least three flights of stairs.

Fortunately, he ended up entering through a window to the upstairs landing and not into her parent's bedroom. Still, he had to find her room. This was a little different than boarding an enemy's ship, being loud in order to frighten them, and knowing, for the most part, where one was going.

Tiptoeing along the darkened hallway, the only thing he knew for certain was her bedroom would be on this level, along with her parents. Above would be any younger siblings for whom there wasn't room on this floor, and farther above them, the lowest class of servants. On the floor below would be the common areas, a drawing room and parlor, and below that, a library and dining room.

Underneath, keeping the entire household afloat, so to speak, was the basement with the kitchen and other servants' areas.

After so long in the trim and compact area of the *Robert*, Philip was still finding the expansive space of London's townhouses, even his own family's, to be almost wasteful.

The layout of this one being so similar to his own, he assumed her parents had the larger room at the back, and Beryl's would be in the front corner overlooking the street. His entire plan gambled upon him being right.

Lifting the latch, he pushed the door open slowly and quietly. The hinges were well oiled and made not a sound. Craning his head around the opening, into the darkened chamber, he could make out a room fit for a young woman, complete with a four-poster bed and a canopy dripping with frills. The gown she'd worn that evening lay carefully across a divan, but he could see little else as the drapes were pulled closed except for a small gap.

Thank God for that gap and the moonlight, or it would be pitch black in there like the hold of a ship!

Drawing a matchbox from his pocket, he quickly lit a match. Yes, it was the right gown. Glancing at the bed, he knew the figure in it to be Beryl.

Shaking out the tiny flame, he crossed to the curtains, drawing them back to allow enough moonlight to stream in so it appeared nearly daylight from the Persian rug to the intricate crown molding adorning the ceiling.

Still, she didn't stir. That's what champagne and dancing until one in the morning would do to a person. As to himself, heart pounding at the atrocity of breaking into a London aristocrat's home, Philip felt entirely alert.

There was nothing to do but awaken her as gently as possible and pray to Poseidon he could prevent her screaming. First, he returned to the door and locked it. If he were to be found out, he wanted a little warning, if only through the rattling of the latch. Perhaps he would jump out the front window to the street below if need be.

The idea of breaking his bones and lying on the pavement was not appealing, and he hoped he could get this over with and escape before the first servants arose and began their duties.

To that end, Philip approached her bed. She was on her side facing the far wall. Rounding the bed, he reached over and touched her shoulder while saying her name.

"Beryl."

She mumbled something.

"Beryl," he tried again. "Don't be alarmed."

Even with the warning, as soon as her eyes opened, her mouth did, too. Prepared for such a reaction, Philip clamped his hand over her mouth, kneeling on the bed to keep himself steady.

She started to thrash, probably still having trouble realizing who he was.

"It is I, Philip Carruthers."

She calmed at once.

"I mean you no harm. Do you understand?"

She nodded under his palm, and he released her. Watching as she sucked in a deep gulp of air, he prayed she didn't expel it in a scream of terror. She did not.

Instead, if his eyes didn't deceive him, she smiled.

"What, no rice sack to drag over my head?" she asked, staring up at him from her pillow.

There was her wry sense of humor.

"No, for I'm not planning on kidnapping you." Though the idea of taking her to his ship and never letting her go did have some appeal.

"How did you get in here?" she asked.

A reasonable question. "I climbed up the back of your house."

To his surprise, she giggled.

"That was very wrong of you," she said when she got ahold of herself. "You could have been injured, and if you had entered my parents' room, you might have been shot."

"My thoughts exactly, and it would have been your fault."

She sat up. "How can you say your behavior is my fault?"

Suddenly, his mouth went dry and his mind, blank. She was a vision with her hair in a thick braid across her shoulder, her rich brown eyes open wide, her lips parted, awaiting his answer.

And wearing only a pale pink nightgown with satin trim. It clung to her full breasts, and he could plainly see the outline of her nipples.

Blimey!

"Captain?" she prompted at his silence.

He hoped he wasn't drooling, but all he could do was stare.

Then, realizing her state of undress, she crossed her arms over her glorious bosom.

Pity! He thought he had been able to detect a hint of dusky pink buds through her nightgown, and now the entire tantalizing view was hidden.

"I want you to leave my chamber at once. Do you realize the damage to my reputation if we were found out?"

It was his turn to laugh.

"You were on board a Chinese junk with fifteen pirates, and then aboard my ship for days with a crew of twenty-seven, including me, whose cabin you slept in. And *now* you're worrying about your reputation?"

She raised her chin. "My father asked me if anything untoward happened, and I assured him it hadn't. And that was the end of it. My reputation is entirely unsullied."

But Philip *had* sullied it. He'd taken her lips in a glorious kiss, and if given the chance, he would sully her some more. Indeed, he wanted to sully her rather badly at that very moment.

It would be no matter at all to lean a little closer and claim her lips. She was already in bed. He remembered exactly how warm and pliable she could be. Surely, he could make her that way again, and then seduce her before first light. There was only a whisper-thin garment between them, after all.

However, he was ultimately a gentleman.

"Where is the necklace? I'm not leaving without it."

She nodded. "Yes, you are."

He wanted to tear his hair out.

"I have told you I was on a mission for Queen Victoria, and the mission isn't over until I fulfill her charge and deliver the necklace to her. I must be the one to do it so I can pay my crew."

"That may be true, or it may be a fantastical lie." She smoothed the bedclothes under her fingers. Then she fixed him with her gaze. "Do you have it in writing?"

"As a matter of fact, I do. I have a letter of marque from her."

She nodded, looking quite reasonable and nonplussed for a young lady conducting negotiations from her bed.

"Then I will see you tomorrow. We shall meet at an appointed place. *Not* my bedroom. You bring the letter, and I'll bring the necklace."

He considered. It was nearly tomorrow in any case. *What could a few hours matter?*

"I suppose you are a woman of your word."

"I am," she agreed. "Besides, what choice do you have?"

He wished she hadn't challenged him like that.

"I could ransack your room in pirate fashion until I discover my treasure."

"And bring the household down upon your head," she reminded him.

"I could ransack quietly," Philip assured her.

That elicited a smile from her, a beautiful smile which spurred him to another thought.

"I could kiss you into acquiescing to my demands."

Her eyes seemed to flash in the moonlight, and he held his breath, awaiting her answer.

She licked her lips, and he nearly groaned aloud.

"You could try," she dared, her voice a soft, husky whisper.

Oh, yes! If that wasn't an invitation, Philip didn't know what was.

Without hesitation, for he didn't know how he'd even waited that long to touch her, he snaked a hand to the back of her head, anchoring her in place, and then he kissed her.

As soon as his mouth touched hers, desire pumped through his veins. By the way she parted her lips allowing him to deepen the kiss, she surely felt the same way.

Pushing her back onto her bed, Philip covered her body with his, resting on his forearms so as not to crush her, continuing to dance with her tongue.

Tasting Beryl's sweetness, he remembered the essence of her, how powerfully enticing she was, even when utterly bedraggled on the *Robert*. She was even more so now they lay upon clean sheets with a light floral scent clinging to her hair and skin.

When her hands grasped his shoulders, holding him in place, he felt like a king. Sucking her lower lip into his mouth, caressing it, nibbling it, he reveled in her soft moans.

And then he dipped his head, trailing kisses along her jaw, down her slender neck which she arched below him, exposing her pulse at its base.

He could feel her heart pounding as fast and fierce as his own.

Across her smooth skin, he left a fluttering caress of his tongue along her collarbone and downward, over the swells of her bosom, and finally, into the valley between. She was writhing under him, her hands now fisting in his hair.

Using his teeth, he dragged the thin, soft neckline of her nightgown downward.

Easily, it gave way, exposing her breasts to his gaze, and then to his mouth.

With the gentlest of licks, his tongue lathed her nipples, then he began to suck in earnest, and as he did, he felt her hips rise beneath him.

"*Mm,*" she moaned.

His groin was aching with need for her. But she was a lady of the *ton. Could he satisfy her without stealing her virginity?* He aimed to try.

To that end, he rolled off her, feeling the sting as her fingers tore at his hair. Her eyelids opened, and she gazed up at him, looking mussed and beautiful.

"Don't go," she murmured, mistaking his movement. "I need . . . you."

Thinking of the precariousness of his position in her room with dawn looming in a few hours, servants awakening, London's streets coming to life outside, he hastened to draw up the bottom of her nightdress.

With the glimmer of moonshine, he could see her clearly, the pale skin of her ankles, then her calves, and lastly, her smooth thighs. Naked beneath her nightdress, she was bathed in white luminescence, including the soft curls over her sweet mound.

He had to touch her. When he smoothed his hand over her flat stomach and onto her curls, her hips pressed upward.

"Relax, sweet lady," he whispered. Then he dipped his finger between her folds and stroked her.

"Oh," she intoned, and her beautiful eyes closed again.

She was damp to his touch. Amazed at her passion, he continued to stroke her, gently at first, then quickening his speed as her hips bucked under his hand. It was one of the most sensual moments he'd ever had, watching her face as she experienced his caress.

Leaning over her while continuing his handiwork, he drew her nipple into his mouth, sucking the hardened tip.

"Philip," she said, her head thrashing. "Yes!"

And apparently, he'd pushed her over the edge. With another cry, which he quickly smothered with his mouth upon hers, she released for him, climaxing easily, her muscles continuing to tighten and ease as long as he stroked her.

Finally, when she relaxed onto the bed, sighing her pleasure, he removed his hand.

She stared up at him.

"You *are* a pirate," were her first words.

He grinned despite his hardened shaft pressing painfully against his pants.

"Maybe I am. Now, will you give me the necklace?"

"No." Reaching up, she pulled his mouth again to hers and initiated another kiss.

"*Mm,*" she hummed.

As it turned out, she'd become quite skilled at kissing. In turn, she licked the seam of his lips, and when he opened his mouth, she thrust her tongue inside, echoing what he had done.

It was thrilling to have a woman plunder his mouth.

When at last Beryl drew back, she said, "I feel so exhausted, but in an exhilarated way."

"I feel so frustrated," Philip confessed, "in a frustrated way."

She giggled.

"I'm sorry," she said, not sounding sorry at all. "I know enough to understand that was only half the act." She gestured at him. "Because your trousers are still on."

He barked out a laugh at her basic understanding of "the act," as she called it.

"It's even better when one does the whole thing," he promised, "but then you couldn't call yourself an innocent any longer or go to your wedding day declaring yourself pure for your groom."

Her marrying anyone seemed a terrible idea, putting him instantly in a foul mood, no doubt fueled by his unsatisfied body.

His disposition only darkened further when she gasped and said, "Arthur!"

Arthur? "Who?"

"My fiancé," she said in a whisper. "The viscount, Lord Arthur Wharton."

Was Philip dim-witted, slow, a fool? How was it this was the first he'd known of a fiancé? He recalled the man he'd seen her with earlier at the Mallory's ball.

Of course, a woman such as Miss Beryl Angsley would be engaged. The only wonder was she wasn't married already. He had assumed, though, if she had such a bond, she wouldn't have sailed halfway around the world.

And he was lying with her in her bed. Moreover, he'd just laid hands upon her person. And lips. And tongue. He almost felt sorry for Wharton.

Philip had to remind himself what had brought him to her house.

It most assuredly hadn't been to kiss Beryl and make her climax. Had it?

"Is the necklace safe?" he asked finally.

Though he'd only seen it for a moment on the pirate junk, its rare, breathtaking beauty had imprinted itself on his memory. At that moment, he could easily imagine it draped around Beryl's slender neck, the pearls dangling over her luscious breasts—equally breathtaking.

At the thought, his shaft grew hard again, feeling as long as a mizzenmast. Quickly rising from her bed, Philip had to put a little distance between himself and this siren of a woman so his body could calm down.

"It is safe," she said, covering herself, drawing her gown down. "I learned about hiding things from my experience on your ship."

What a strange thing to say!

He sighed. The time on his ship was in the past. They were home, and she was going to marry a viscount. The sooner he got out of her life, the better.

"Very well," he ground out. "Where and when? It is nearly dawn. Shall we meet before or after the midday meal?"

"When I said tomorrow, I meant *tomorrow*, as in *not* this day though it still feels like last night, does it not?"

"You are speaking in riddles. Are you stalling?" he asked. *Would she hang onto the necklace to keep him in her life?*

Shaking his head at his own fanciful hopes, he waited, hands on his hips.

"Tomorrow," Beryl repeated. "My mother would think it strange for me to rush out today after getting home so late. When not the high Season, we normally rest indoors the day after a ball. If she asks questions, I would have to lie to her, and I don't like to lie."

She stared pointedly at him. *Did she think he was lying about something?*

"Moreover, if it is much later this afternoon, my mother will want to go with me."

That wouldn't do. *How would he kiss her again at their next meeting if her mother were lingering about?*

Avast, he told himself. If he'd harbored any notion that he could somehow win the heart and hand of Miss Angsley—and, in truth, he *had* fantasized about it—he now realized its absurdity. She was engaged to a peer of the realm.

They had to conclude this necklace business between them, and then he had to vow to leave her alone. At that moment, though, he wished he could simply stand there all day and look at her, with her cheeks flushed, eyes sparkling, hair mussed. She looked entirely delectable, despite being an infuriating minx.

"Once more, then, I ask where and when?"

CHAPTER ELEVEN

"St. Paul's Cathedral?" Beryl considered aloud, but then she thought of a better place. "No, St. James's Park. Duck Island. My mother knows I love to go see the pelicans. I'll be there at one o'clock tomorrow."

Was it silly she couldn't wait for time to pass until then?

"And you will bring the paper to prove recovering the necklace was your charge from the queen?" she insisted.

"The letter of marque states I'm sanctioned by Queen Victoria. It doesn't mention the necklace."

"I see." *Was he playing with her?*

Philip shook his head. "I don't care for the doubtful tone to your voice, nor your frown."

Reaching toward her, he caressed her forehead, smoothing it.

"I can prove it was my mission," he added. "Listen, and I'll say this as briefly and plainly as possible, and then I had best be off before I compromise you and we have to marry."

She shrugged, maintaining a placid expression when inside, her heartbeat had sped up at his words. *What if they had to marry? Would he be upset at the prospect?*

For an instant, she thought it would be fortuitous if one of her parents happened along. Then she considered the shame and how it would disappoint them. And, of course, there was Arthur.

Sitting up in bed, she clutched her satin counterpane to her chest, watching his eyes follow her movements. *How would he prove the necklace was not simply pirate booty he'd happened upon in China?*

"Tell me," she urged, "and then, as you said, you must go."

"The gray pearls in the necklace previously belonged to Queen Marie Antoinette, and they were smuggled to England by Elizabeth, Countess of Sutherland, the wife of a British diplomat. The queen of France intended for the countess to keep them only until she escaped The Temple where Marie Antionette was imprisoned with her family, or until loyalists triumphed over the revolution. However, a year later, the queen was headless and could no longer use her jewels. Naturally, the Sutherlands kept them."

"How sad," Beryl said, and she meant it.

Philip shrugged and continued his tale. "Years ago, the Sutherlands used some of the French queen's pearls to create a necklace for one of their brides. The current duchess was at the palace, performing her duties as Mistress of the Robes for our queen. At a state dinner attended by ambassadors to the Qing emperor, she wore the necklace, removing it later that evening in her room at the palace. And that was the last she saw of it."

"Someone pilfered it from the palace," Beryl mused, trying to imagine such audacity. "And because the emperor's emissaries were visiting, naturally, you were sent to China to look for it."

"Exactly. As you can imagine, the Duchess of Sutherland wants her necklace back. Any of Marie Antoinette's jewels are rare, at least in England, though she managed to send the rest to her sister, Marie Christine, in Brussels. Queen Victoria is upset on behalf of her lady-in-waiting, naturally, but more than that, she is angry at someone following the Manchus' orders to steal from Buckingham Palace. It could as easily have been an order to slit our queen's throat, if you see her concern."

"I do, of course," Beryl agreed. "What a fascinating story, Captain. You have certainly earned your necklace."

He smiled.

"Tomorrow," she added, making his smile dim slightly. "With the pelicans. Now, you really must be going."

In fact, she could hear the rag-and-bone man calling his way along the street, which meant servants must be rousing in the basement and the attic.

Instead of hurrying out of her room, he knelt upon her bed, leaned close, and kissed her again.

"Until tomorrow, my lady."

How romantic! Like a Shakespearean play or an Austen novel.

"Until tomorrow, Lord Corsair."

She noticed he rolled his eyes at her use of his nickname.

"I'm starting to feel more like a pirate every day," he muttered and disappeared as quietly as he'd come.

SLEEPING WELL AND RISING after lunch, Beryl was still pondering their pre-dawn tryst—for that's what she'd decided to call it—as her maid helped her dress. Her only regret was in forgetting to ask after Leo, her soft and sweet companion from those long hours in his owner's cabin. She hoped he was well. Even more, if possible, she hoped to see the cat again.

Would the captain remain in her life after she returned the necklace?

Being honest with herself, she wanted him to, though she couldn't see how it would be possible. Not if she remained on her planned path of marriage with Arthur.

On the other hand, she wouldn't have let Philip touch her as he had if his kiss hadn't immediately confirmed her strong feelings for him.

What had begun as a tiny ember of interest had flared to full-blown love. Rash of her, she knew, and no one would understand it, least of all herself, but the man had plundered her heart and taken it for his own.

And it wasn't simply a cherished memory of months ago, embellished by her fertile imagination. It was happening even now. She'd felt as if she were in a daze until the Mallory's ball. That instant, upon seeing Philip again, dancing in his arms, she'd come alive as she hadn't been since parting from him on the deck of the *Robert*.

Even then, thinking of the captain, her body warmed, and low, between her hips, her stomach fluttered when she thought of how he'd touched her and kissed her. Instantly, her nipples puckered at the recollection. She wanted him to touch her and do much more, as well.

What's more, try as she might, she could not conjure these same feelings for Arthur.

She wanted the type of man who could dance a fine waltz one minute and secretly find his way into her bedroom the next to drive her mindless with his mouth and hands. She wanted Philip Carruthers!

When he'd mentioned having to get married if they were caught together, she couldn't dredge up an ounce of regret. Thus, she'd not given him the necklace, the recovery of which clearly was his charge from the queen. Beryl had needed a reason to see him again, and making him meet her on the rather romantic island in the middle of the park might spark the man to words of affection and attachment.

She hoped it was a sunny day.

If he gave her the slightest sign he returned her affection, she would consider ending her engagement with Arthur. At that point, she would deal with her parents' displeasure at her throwing away an advantageous match for a dubious one.

Meanwhile, she had the difficult task of deciding which gown to put on after lunch the next day. *What would please Philip? What would invoke his passion?*

Then she laughed. The captain had seen her bare save for her nightgown bunched around her waist from his maneuverings, both tugging it down—*with his teeth!*—and drawing it up. *Did it matter anymore what she wore to meet him?*

In any case, first thing in the morning, if she could wait that long, she was going to visit Eleanor. How she'd missed her friend's company during the many months she'd been traveling, for it seemed a day didn't go by when she didn't wish to converse with her.

Tomorrow, they would discuss the recent ball, which fashions they had liked and which they hadn't, who seemed to be forming an attachment with whom, and, of course, their many dance partners, as if Beryl could even think of anyone except the captain.

And now she had even more to tell Eleanor, though how much she would reveal of the tryst's exciting activities, she wasn't sure. She would hate to lose her friend's admiration and respect, and she was certain some of what occurred was beyond the pale of decency.

If Eleanor told her of a pre-dawn assignation and of letting a man fondle her naked body, then Beryl supposed she would be shocked, yet supportive. Especially if the heart was involved. Hopefully, Eleanor would feel the same, for Beryl truly needed to discuss her feelings for the captain with her best friend.

Thus, the next morning, not even waiting until the appointed polite hour of ten o'clock, she set out for the Lindsey residence on Portman Square. Eleanor's oldest sister, Jenny, had married Lord Lindsey and become a countess, and her middle sister, Maggie, had married Beryl's own cousin, John Angsley, Lord Cambrey—whom Robert Carruthers had gravely injured. Thus, Maggie was also a countess. And Eleanor lived in the lap of luxury going between the Lindseys at Portman Square and Cavendish Square where the Cambreys had their London townhouse.

Though Eleanor being Eleanor, she said she preferred the Blackwood's cottage in Sheffield, many hours north in the south of Yorkshire. Sometimes her friend was a little odd. But it made her the person she was and whom Beryl loved.

Distracted, thinking happy thoughts, she nearly slid off the carriage seat when it came to a lurching stop. The footman jumped down, coming to the window.

"The road is blocked, miss, by two carriages. Perhaps an accident."

"Oh," she stuck her head out, and could easily see the Lindsey townhouse up ahead. "I shall walk from here."

And she let her father's footman help her down from the carriage a mere block away from Eleanor's front door.

"Will you return in two hours?" she asked him.

"Of course, miss," and he hopped back onto the vehicle.

She watched as her father's driver managed to turn the horses in a perfect U-shape and go back the way they had come. She was early, too early for most visitors to be making calls, and, thus, except for the carriages inexplicably blocking Portman Square, the pavements were empty.

That was precisely why she heard the footsteps behind her—more than one pair.

Unfortunately, she turned too late to see the danger. Too late to scream if there had even been anyone to hear her.

Then the familiar, hated rice sack was lowered over her head, cutting off her sight while a hand clamped over her mouth, stopping the yell for help she was trying to make.

Hell's bells! she swore in a very unladylike fashion, the oath trapped in her head.

Belatedly, she realized the parked carriages had been a trap to get her out of her coach.

Kidnapped again, no doubt by the same Chinese pirates, and this time in the heart of London.

CHAPTER TWELVE

Bloody hell! Philip had waited an hour and then cooled his heels for another half an hour, and his temper grew as his patience dwindled. He'd trusted her to meet him.

In truth, he was surprised, given their last encounter, that Beryl had let him down. She seemed to understand the importance of the necklace and of his returning it to Buckingham Palace, which was only ten minutes as the crow flies at the opposite end of St. James's Park.

Apparently, she'd only been teasing him about giving it back.

Fuming, tired of looking at the ugly pelicans, which Leo found utterly mesmerizing, even more annoyed by the happy families coming to see them, Philip finally returned to his carriage.

Now what?

It was broad daylight so he couldn't return to her room and confront her. However, he also refused to wait until nightfall. Philip decided to settle on the civilized hour of three o'clock, when visitors sometimes appeared unannounced. Too late for lunch, too early for dinner, unexpected guests couldn't be accused of dropping in for a free meal.

At the stroke of three, he knocked on Lord Angsley's front door, grumbling a little to himself. She had better be home and she had better be prepared to see him.

When a sweating, harried butler came into view—*sweat on an unflappable London butler's temple!*—Philip knew something was terribly wrong.

Before he could announce himself, the man opened wide the door, revealing chaos. A maid was weeping by a potted fern. Next to her, a youngster was doing the same. A policeman paced the marble floor, and loud voices could be heard from a room to the left.

Suddenly, that door opened, and a woman, obviously Beryl's mother by the resemblance, came running out, sobbing into a handkerchief and disappeared up the stairs, followed by another maid who was plainly trying to console her.

Philip's heartbeat quickened as he stepped inside. When out of the same room came a constable, followed by Lord Angsley, who was followed in turn by his nephew, the Earl of Cambrey, whom Philip had met once before a few years prior, he could see why the butler was sweating. Trouble was afoot.

The policeman stopped pacing and every eye turned to Philip standing in the foyer, feeling as out of place as a mizzenmast in the middle of the House of Lords.

"What has happened?" he asked, his gut telling him the answer before her father did, for the one person he'd come to see was not evident.

"My daughter is missing."

At his words, the maid cried harder.

But it was the Earl of Cambrey who approached him, his gaze fixed on his.

"What are *you* doing here? What part do you play in this?"

Two reasonable questions which deserved answers.

Before Philip could begin to figure out what to say, Lord Angsley spoke up, "He is the ship's captain who rescued Beryl from the Chinese pirates."

The earl's glance didn't waver. "He is also the brother of the man who died crashing his vehicle into mine."

"What?" Lord Angsley exclaimed.

"Extraordinary," muttered the constable.

Christ!

"That's hardly important now," Philip pointed out. "What has happened to Beryl?"

"*Beryl*, is it?" Cambrey asked, scowling. "You call my cousin by her first name. You didn't answer my questions."

Philip's mind was whirling, yet he kept coming up with the same thought: *Chui-A-poo.*

"Are you involved in this, Captain?" her father asked, his expression grim.

"In a way, I suppose I am. I'm here because your daughter took something from my cabin, something very valuable. She was supposed to meet me today to return it. When she didn't, I came here."

"I see," Lord Angsley said, sounding defeated.

The constable clucked in disapproval.

"Well, I don't bloody see," the earl intoned, his voice harsh and accusing. "Why would she take something from you, and how did you arrange to meet her? And why would that make her disappear?"

Lady Angsley had reappeared at the top of the stairs, and her sobbing joined that of the maids.

"May we retire to your parlor?" Philip asked.

The constable looked at Lord Angsley, who looked at Lord Cambrey, who nodded and turned on his heel. Philip drew a deep breath and followed them. He'd rather hoped Lady Angsley with her tragic sobbing, which only increased his abject dread for Beryl's safety, would remain upstairs. Instead, she hurried down and trailed in behind them, thankfully without the crying maid or child.

Succinctly, Philip explained about his mission for the queen and how Beryl assumed he was a pirate and thus *liberated* the jewels from his cabin. Even more briefly, he said she'd agreed to meet him to return the necklace.

No need to mention scaling the outside of the house like a ship's mast.

"A necklace?" her father said. "I suppose that has something to do with why this was left on our doorstep." He drew from his pocket the gold chain with the green stone, which Philip had last seen in Chui-A-poo's hands.

He felt the blood drain from his head as the man passed it over to him.

"I hadn't seen it since we were in the Orient," her father added.

"I last saw it in the pirate leader's hands," Philip admitted. "He—or most likely, his men—have abducted her."

He said the words calmly, knowing in his gut Chui had sent men halfway around the world to reclaim at least one treasure. Or perhaps both.

The Earl of Cambrey made an exasperated sound. "I've had about enough of you and your family! You got her caught up in this mess."

Philip could see it from the other man's point of view, but he was wrong.

"Beryl's traipsing across China is what attracted Chui-A-poo, the pirate. To him, she is an exotic western beauty. He wants her for his wife."

Lady Angsley cried out in denial.

"However, he also wants the Duchess of Sutherland's necklace, which, as I said, I had in my possession and Beryl took. Do you have any idea where it is?" Philip asked her father.

Lord Angsley shook his head.

"Did they take her directly from your home?" Philip asked, wondering if anyone had seen how he'd entered from the back alley and had done the same.

"No, Captain," said Lady Angsley, speaking her first coherent words. "My daughter went to visit her friend Miss Blackwood this morning. Our driver dropped her off. When he went back for her, he found out she'd never made it inside her destination."

She hiccupped back another sob.

Philip could only imagine how her mother would have reacted had she been in Stanley when Beryl was kidnapped the first time.

"Was there anything else on your doorstep?" Philip asked. There had to be a message as to how Chui-A-poo wanted the necklace delivered.

"Beryl's necklace was wrapped in *white* silk." Lord Angsley's voice was rough with emotion, and he shared a private glance with Philip, both men understanding China— one as a diplomat, one as a privateer. The use of the somber, threatening white, indicating purity and death, was no accident.

"He doesn't want her hurt," Philip assured her parents.

Though Chui-A-poo might want the necklace more than he needed another wife, in which case—

"There was also this, tied to her necklace." Her father handed a piece of rice paper to Philip. "It made no sense until you told us she has the duchess's necklace in her possession. My nephew had it translated on the docks by midday," he added, nodding toward the earl.

Philip studied it. Underneath words in Peking dialect, written in a wavering script, it read, "Captain bring pearl necklace to ship. Dawn."

"I suppose *you* are the captain they refer to," the Earl of Cambrey said, his tone beyond irritated.

Philip nodded slowly. "And I suppose I am to meet the kidnappers on my ship." *With the candlestick and the cat for support!*

"Perhaps we can all hide on board, overpower them, and get my daughter back," Lord Angsley suggested.

The constable made a scoffing sound. "I can send policemen to the captain's vessel," he suggested.

Philip narrowed his eyes and tapped his chin. "I cannot imagine they will bring her to my ship. She's hidden somewhere, probably Pennyfields or Limehouse Causeway," he said, thinking of the two dockside areas with the largest populations of Chinese.

"How will we ever find her?" Lady Angsley asked, standing and wrapping her arms around herself for comfort.

The earl had been silent throughout their exchange. "I believe I can locate her."

They all looked at him. "There is one thing that motivates most people," Cambrey declared. "Money. Luckily, I have a lot of it. Moreover, I have some experience with a substance the Chinese both love and loathe— opium."

At their continued stares, the earl shrugged. "Excuse the vulgar discussion, Auntie," he said to Lady Angsley. "But you all know the wealth to be had over the opium trade. Some Chinese are bitter at how the British seem to be making the lion's share. They are even angrier at their own coastal pirates helping the English merchants smuggle opium inland against their government's wishes. Basically, the pirates are betraying their countrymen for coin."

"And you know some of these bitter Chinese in London?" Philip asked.

Who would have thought the Earl of Cambrey, priggishly outraged by Philip using Beryl's first name, was familiar with the seedier side of the opium trade?

"I do," the earl acknowledged. "They also make fine silk, of which my wife is very fond. The money I used to spend on opium, I now spend on what pleases my countess. In any case, the communities are comparatively small. If an English woman has been kidnapped by Chinese pirates and is being held, I can guarantee you half of the Chinamen at the docks know about it already."

"Regardless," Lord Angsley pointed out, "it seems we need the necklace. Either to trade or as insurance."

"I will leave that to you," Cambrey said and headed for the door. "After all, he's practically a pirate." He gestured at Philip. "Finding treasure is his forte. He found the necklace once. I'm sure he can do it again. And I'll do my best to discover my cousin's whereabouts. Constable, I suppose you may come with me as there is little for you to do here."

In their wake, those who were left, looked grim-faced at one another.

It didn't sit well with Philip to have the Earl of Cambrey out searching for Beryl while he stayed behind. Recalling the moment he'd burst into the pirate captain's cabin and discovered her the first time, looking beautiful and afraid, he longed to rescue her again. Maybe it was the code he'd discussed with Rufus—saving her life made him feel responsible for her forever.

Rubbish! He loved her!

To wipe away any traces of fear and to kiss her until she smiled again, those were the thoughts distracting him from caring about recovering the duchess's necklace.

That he might never see Beryl again was unthinkable.

"Her bedroom is the best place to search," her mother offered.

Would he be invited abovestairs to help?

"I'll show you the way," she added.

Apparently, he was. Following her mother upstairs, her father trailing behind, Philip considered the last time he was in her room. He'd had the distinct feeling she had kept the necklace there with her.

Then her words came back to him. *I learned about hiding things from my experience on your ship.*

"Does she have a trunk or a chest?" Philip asked, as they entered her bedroom.

Her mother shook her head, surveying the empty chamber and looking as though she might start crying again.

"No. She thinks such a thing at the end of the bed clutters the room."

For his part, Philip couldn't even look at the bed, not without picturing her laid bare before him, passionate, desirable, satiated. A lump formed in his throat.

Then, they began to search.

Glancing around, he spied the tall wardrobe and thought of his hiding place for brandy. In two strides, he yanked the doors open, confronted with her gowns. Pushing them aside as best he could, breathing in her familiar floral scent, he felt around at the back. But he'd had a shelf in his wardrobe. Hers was full length and overflowing with dresses. Moreover, he couldn't even see the bottom of it.

And she worried about the clutter of a trunk?

Ignoring her parents who were searching elsewhere, her mother going through her chest of drawers and her father looking over and under furniture, he began pulling out her gowns and tossing them to the floor beside him. When her wardrobe was empty, he was on his hands and knees, feeling around among the dropped ribbons and lace fichus, a misplaced dancing slipper and a few silk stockings, finding nothing.

While her mother rehung the gowns, Philip spent another hour helping her father to roll back the carpet, then to look behind the drapes, and even tore her bed apart. Still, no necklace. Then Lady Angsley began to search inside each of her daughter's shoes, and her father wondered aloud if they would need to search the entire house, which would take more time than they had.

Running his hands through his hair, Philip considered how she'd taken the necklace off his ship. She'd had nothing but—

The gown!

Soon, he was rummaging through her clothing again, pushing aside brocade and cotton, satin and silk.

"Captain, what on earth—?" her mother began.

"I've found it!" Philip said in triumph.

"The necklace?" her father asked.

"The gown she was wearing on my ship. I bought it for her myself."

Standing up, he hefted its weight, feeling how the hem pulled down beyond the heaviness of the pale green silk skirt.

"I think the necklace is here. It's sewn into the hem."

Sliding a knife out of his boot—catching her father's surprised expression—Philip slit the stitches open. The necklace was suddenly cast upon the Persian carpet, a cascade of diamonds, rubies, and distinctly gray pearls.

Her mother gasped.

Tossing the gown aside, Philip bent to pick it up, holding it before their eyes. Her father whistled at the fine craftmanship and beauty.

"I can see why everyone wants it," he said. "But it's nothing compared to my Beryl."

"Agreed!" Philip dropped it into his coat pocket. "We don't have long before the sun sets. When we get Beryl back, we still need to dispatch the pirates. If we let them stay, they will only kidnap her again or try to."

Her father was already walking toward the door. "I appreciate your firm belief we will get her back."

Philip swallowed. "The alternative, my lord, is unthinkable."

Lord Angsley led the way downstairs, back into the parlor where, so much like her daughter, Lady Angsley requested tea, and Philip told them how Beryl had demanded tea, sitting on the deck of his ship in the sunshine.

Her mother gave him a watery smile.

"We have only two choices," her father stated. "We can capture these pirates so this Chui person never hears from them again. Hopefully, he will give up when his men do not return. Or we can kill them."

Philip considered the tenaciousness of Chui-A-poo, sending a ship all the way to England.

"I don't think he will admit defeat if he hears nothing. He might assume they never reached Britain. I believe he would try again, and we would never know when his men might appear. Even if we kill them, he will still send more. He has an endless supply in his fleet, I assure you."

Lord Angsley rubbed his temples. "Then what do you suggest?"

"Truly, I believe you should ask the queen to send men to China to kill him or, at the very least, to request the Qing government help capture him."

Then, Philip had another idea. "Or, since we're dealing with pirates, I suppose we could take the measure of his men and see if they will turn mutineer for a generous fee. For enough coin, they might return to China and capture their leader. They could get a reward from us and hand him over to the British on Hong Kong Island for another handsome bounty."

Lord Angsley steepled his fingers.

"I will consider what you say. As a diplomat, I cannot ask our queen to order his assassination, but paying his own men to turn on him, that's another story."

Philip nodded. "They are pirates after all, and it's the way of pirates to shift allegiance like the sands move with the tides. First, we have to meet with them."

"And we can't do so," her father pondered, "until Beryl is safe."

A man of action, Lord Angsley penned a letter to the foreign affairs secretary, notifying him of his daughter's kidnapping and suggesting, as Philip had said, that the queen consider some action toward the pirate leader known as Chui-A-poo.

Sealing this, he gave it to the policeman who still uselessly patrolled the foyer, sending him at once to the Houses of Parliament.

"I should send word to Lord Wharton," Lady Angsley said, exchanging a glance with her husband.

"Beryl's fiancé," her father clarified, though Philip had recalled the name immediately.

What that sallow, namby-pamby gentleman could do to help the situation was beyond him. However, if she were his, Philip would certainly want to know she was in danger. Thus, he sat idly by as Lady Angsley penned a note to Beryl's beloved and sent it off with the red-nosed maid who managed to dry her eyes enough to do her mistress's bidding.

Unfortunately, there was nothing more they could do except wait for word from the Earl of Cambrey, knowing all the while, even if they hadn't found her, Philip would go to his ship at first light and meet the pirates.

Without Beryl, he would have no choice but to hand the necklace over. And then, they might lose both treasures.

Finally, close to sunset, a noise in the hallway heralded Lord Cambrey's return. Philip was on his feet even before the parlor door was thrust open.

"Any news?" Lord Angsley asked his nephew.

The earl grinned. "I've found her!"

⚭

CHAPTER THIRTEEN

Miss Beryl Angsley had had about enough of this nonsense. One night, she was at a ball and drinking champagne, and the next, she was lying on a bunk in a squalid room that smelled like the fishiest fish with a guard seated nearby, silent and sullen.

Even if he spoke, she doubted they would understand each other.

If the Chinaman's eyes hadn't been open, she would have thought he was asleep for all the expression he had. She'd tried to converse with him after he had removed the sack from her head—the blasted rice bag!

Again, her hair looked as if she'd been standing on board ship in a strong wind and then rolled around in a rice patty. She was still picking the little grains out from what was left of her braided and coiled bun.

Moreover, she had just awakened again from another fitful dream to find she was still in the strange place with her silent guard with his long black queue and his red cap. And it was dark out. Whether it was closer to midnight or dawn, she couldn't tell. She thought it was still the night of the same day during which she'd intended to visit Eleanor, the day she would have met Philip by the pelicans. However, she wasn't certain.

It made her want to cry, except she had no tears.

She tried again. "Water. May I please have some water?"

Her guard continued to look straight ahead, blinking occasionally.

She pointed to her mouth, then stuck out her tongue, which felt dry.

"I'm thirsty," she said. "See, I fear my tongue is swelling."

If only this eternal night would end. Maybe in the daylight, someone else would come in. Or maybe things would get worse.

She didn't really care about her grumbling stomach, but she was thirsty.

"Water," she said again. At least her hands weren't tied. Whoever captured her probably considered she was no match for a man, so why bother restraining her? Especially when this brute didn't close his eyes for even a moment.

Sitting up, she pantomimed choking herself, putting her hands around her own neck, coughing and gagging, then held her hand up as if drinking from a glass.

Nothing. The man didn't even raise an eyebrow. *What a fiend!*

Rolling to her feet, she stood. That got a reaction out of him. He, too, surged to his feet. Sighing, Beryl wondered what she hoped to gain.

Her freedom, for one! Wouldn't it be nice if she could save herself and wander back home to tell the tale? However, looking around for a weapon, she spied not even a candlestick. There was no fireplace, so no fireirons, though there was a brick area which appeared to be used for cooking. Directly above it, a hole had been chopped in the roof.

Cooking without a chimney? She couldn't imagine the dangerous conditions.

It was obviously a poor family's home. There was another bed, taking up most of the space, a small table at which the Chinese pirate sat, and an even smaller shrine in the corner with a buddha and some incense sticks such as she'd seen in the Orient.

Unless she could grab a brick and chuck it at her captor, there was nothing of use to her.

Would he stop her from exercising her legs? In truth, she thought she could sleep again but feared the frightening dreams, and she dreaded awakening to find nothing had changed.

With that in mind, Beryl took a few tentative steps toward the table. The man scowled, but there wasn't really anywhere else to walk, so she circled the table, glancing at the door. Then she rounded the back of his pushed-out chair, close enough now he could reach out and grab her if he wanted.

As he turned, she noted a long knife handle protruding from the top of his pants, his queue dangling over it.

Shivering with the idea of the wicked blade, she passed him, heading toward the window with no covering except a tattered . . . rice sack? She nearly laughed.

Glancing out into the darkness, she could see the faintest lightening of the sky in the distance, but the fingers of dawn had yet to crest the horizon.

Was that what they were waiting for? Enough light to sail away? Would she be taken aboard a junk and forced to return to the Orient?

The notion of a long voyage surrounded by pirates who couldn't speak to her and seemed to think she needed neither food nor water, nor a privy for that matter, caused her terror to build.

Her guard was close behind her now. Even without words, she sensed standing by a window where she might be seen was the cause of his movement. Any second, he would probably lay hands on her and drag her away from it.

Could she break through the panes and hurl herself down to the street below?

Her body would undoubtedly sustain great injury, perhaps mortal.

Peering down to gauge the distance, with her eyes growing accustomed to the darkness, she spied the outline of a cat sitting in the street, fluffy and stout. Whether he was orange, she couldn't see, but in her heart, she was certain of it. If Leo was there, then Philip was, too.

With anticipation raising the hair on her neck, Beryl turned abruptly, nearly bumping into the guard, who was only a shade taller than her but well-muscled as were all the sailors she'd encountered.

They locked gazes as she eased around him and returned to her place on the bed.

Sitting upright, hands on her lap, feet on the floor, she waited for history to repeat itself.

"THE FAMILY WASN'T TOO thrilled about being displaced. They were paid enough to do it but not enough to keep quiet about it." Lord Cambrey had uttered those words in Lord Angsley's parlor, and then the three men had taken off for the Chinese district of Limehouse, just past Whitechapel.

Lord Angsley had armed himself and lent a pistol to Cambrey, and Philip had his pepperbox revolver concealed under his civilized London coat, with extra shot in his pocket.

As they jumped into Cambrey's coach, Beryl's father exclaimed in surprise when Leo leaped in, even as he was closing the door.

"What in the hell?" Cambrey asked, as the cat sat on the seat, staring out the window, unbothered by the occupants.

"My cat," Philip bit out, feeling sheepish. He hoped to say no more on the matter, but both men were staring at him, clearly confounded.

"He keeps company with me," he added. "If he hadn't made it inside, he would have ridden on the roof. He prefers the interior."

Glancing at his brother's cat, he lifted his hand to stroke it, but the cat's head whipped around, daring him, and his tail flashed.

Thinking better of it, Philip dropped his hand to his lap. The only person since Robert who could touch its soft fur without injury was Beryl.

"The cat took a liking to your daughter when she was on my ship," he finished lamely, as if that explained everything.

Cambrey stared at Leo with more interest. "Do you think it knows we are this very minute traveling to rescue her?"

"Don't be absurd!" Lord Angsley said, but they all continued to look at the feline, who began to wash its paws and face as if preparing for . . . battle.

The journey to Limehouse and into the heart of the docks area of Limehouse Hole, where the Isle of Dogs jutted out into the Thames, seemed to take an eternity. In reality, with the streets being empty at five o'clock in the morning, their ride took less than half an hour.

"Your driver didn't spare the horses," Philip said with appreciation as they got out of Cambrey's carriage a block away from where Beryl was being held over a fishmonger's shop. He watched while Leo sauntered along the street in the dim light, sitting down on the pavement as if he'd been designated the lookout.

They had a short window of time. They needed the cover of darkness but not the pitch-black of night when terrible mistakes could be made. As long as it wasn't sunrise, they weren't too late.

They'd discussed the plan during the journey. Knowing from the Chinese sailor, who worked for the East India Company and who'd accepted a handsome amount from Cambrey to tell him everything, only three pirates were there. The rest were on board the junk at the nearby Limehouse docks.

Lord Angsley would stay on the street in case any of the pirates escaped with Beryl, whereas Cambrey and Philip would reach her via two routes. The earl was going through the fishmonger's, breaking in as it wasn't yet open and then rushing up the stairs. Philip was scaling the back of the building, and, to that end, he quickly disappeared into the alley.

His heart was thumping as if he were boarding an enemy's vessel with cannons exploding and pistols firing. The stakes were far higher than any adventure he'd had in China, except when he found Beryl the first time. He simply hadn't realized then how important this woman would become to him.

Now, she was the greatest treasure he'd ever gone after.

The back of the building had no trellis to assist him, but he was near the docks and this was a sailor's home. The man knew the dangers to his family of being trapped on the second floor. Thus, a crude ladder made of thick, knotted rope dangled from above, where there was not a proper balcony so much as a wooden ledge. No doubt the sailor's wife hung her laundry from it on dry days.

For Philip, it was nothing to climb and gain access to the two-room home, as he'd been told it was. Trying to peer inside, however, through the grimy window, half covered in cloth was pointless. If he jimmied it open, it would take too long and make too much noise, alerting any pirates on the other side.

With a deep breath, using his shoulder and foot, he simply crashed through the window, revolver drawn.

Everything happened at once. He heard a scream from the next room—Beryl! He saw two men arise from mats on the floor, their weapons coming out as they did. Then Cambrey broke in the door from the stairwell, and the pirates' attention was divided.

Hearing the click of a trigger, he started shooting at the same times as each of the other men in the room.

As always happened in a battle, Philip waited to feel hot lead tear through his flesh. When it didn't, and the gunfire stopped, the earl was still standing on the other side of the room and the pirates were writhing on the floor.

After Beryl's scream, there'd been only silence from the next room. If she wasn't alone, her captor had been given all the warning he needed. Nodding to Cambrey, Philip did the only thing he could think of, he broke the door down.

The room was empty.

How in blue blazes?

It took only a moment to see the outline of a trapdoor to the fishmonger's below, situated in the middle of the floor, a common enough apparatus for when the room had been storage instead of a family's living quarters. A table that must have stood over it, was now tipped on its side.

Bloody Hell!

"She's gone," he said to Cambrey.

Flinging the hatch open, Philip slid down the ladder below. As his feet hit the sawdust of the shop floor, he heard the earl behind him. The two of them went crashing into the street.

It was deserted, save for Lord Angsley a few yards down and Leo on the crude wooden sidewalk directly opposite. In a flash, the cat crossed the street, running like the lion he was named for, slipping past both men and into the alley.

"Which way did they go?" the earl yelled toward his uncle.

"They didn't come out!" Lord Angsley returned.

Philip and Cambrey stared at each other a moment.

"We've been tricked," Philip said, turning and running back into the fishmonger's. Over his shoulder, he added, "We should've known Beryl couldn't get down a ladder that quickly, not in a dress."

Like a monkey, Philip scampered up the ladder and back into the room above. Then he saw it, a panel in the wall gaped open.

"Dammit! She was right here the whole time."

"Not anymore," Cambrey said, dodging past him to the other room where the pirates remained, either passed out from loss of blood or dead.

"Go right!" Philip yelled, and the earl hurried to the broken window.

Cambrey climbed out on the wooden ledge, and Philip was directly behind him. Then, for the first time in an eternity, he saw her, though in the dim light before dawn she was merely a shape. Beryl was being dragged along by her arms toward the end of the alley, kicking and struggling the entire way.

Unfortunately, it wasn't making a bit of difference. The pirate continued as if she were no more than a flopping fish, a nuisance but not a deterrent. Once they went out into the warren of small streets and doorways of Limehouse Hole, Philip would lose her forever.

The earl was already on the rope ladder climbing down, but Philip couldn't wait. The love of his life was about to vanish, and there would be no point to his life if she did so.

"Sorry," he muttered to Cambrey as he climbed onto the ladder, too, and when he reached the earl's shoulders, he slid down the man's back and jumped the rest of the way. Then Philip began to run as if the hounds of hell were at his heels.

Hearing the noise behind him, the pirate quickened his pace, hampered by Beryl's flailing gown and arms.

Chasing him nearly to the alley's end, Philip decided he'd have to risk taking a shot, though the distance was far and the narrow lane between the buildings was even darker than the street.

He'd spent three shots in the small room, leaving him three more. Without breaking stride, he fired, thinking to warn the man by shooting into the ground to his right. The man didn't hesitate.

Philip dared not aim too far left in case he hit her. Firing another shot, he missed again.

And then the pirate stopped short, with Beryl crashing into him and her captor nearly losing hold of her.

Philip couldn't see what was at the end of the alley until he was a mere ten feet behind. Then he saw him—Leo, puffed up to twice his size, standing sideways in a perfect arch, tail like a flue brush, and hissing like oil on a flaming fire.

"*Móguǐ!*" yelled the pirate, which Philip knew meant either devil or demon.

True enough, Leo looked as though he could be both.

In the blink of an eye, the cat ran and leaped upon the pirate, undoubtedly shredding the man's shirt as he climbed his body to his head, knocking off his cap in the process.

Releasing Beryl, who staggered backward and fell to the ground, the Chinaman was scrabbling with both hands to pull off the animal.

Philip aimed but hesitated. After all, Beryl was safe, and there was no reason to kill the man. Then, still screaming and frantically clawing at Leo, the pirate reached behind, grabbing for the knife handle protruding from his cloth belt.

"I've got her," Cambrey assured him, and out of the corner of his eye, Philip saw the earl helping his cousin to her feet.

And then the blade was in the pirate's hand, and Philip, with only one shot remaining, fired.

CHAPTER FOURTEEN

Time seemed to stand still for the briefest of moments as Philip lowered his weapon.

Leo jumped to safety, landing easily on his four paws as the pirate fell, perhaps mortally wounded. Philip briefly wondered if charges could be brought against him for killing a man to protect a cat.

He felt not a trace of guilt. He'd been unable to save his twin, who'd died alone on a cobbled street in another part of London, but at least, he'd saved Robert's cat.

Then his gaze took in Beryl's disheveled but otherwise unhurt appearance. She'd pulled a wadded gag from her mouth, which she now dropped to her feet where Leo was already circling and getting under her skirts. Obviously, it had been the only way to keep her quiet in the hidey-hole.

Philip didn't give a damn the earl would see what happened next. In quick steps, he tore Beryl from her cousin's grasp and gathered her into his arms.

Holding her tightly, feeling her heart beating, strong and brisk, against his chest, Philip found his eyes filling with tears and his throat closing with emotion. Only then did he acknowledge the terror he'd been harboring.

And at that moment, the anguish and guilt he'd felt for the past four years, every time he'd considered how Robert had died, lifted.

What's more, Robert's cat had clearly chosen Beryl for him, and then helped to save her, and in Philip's gut, he believed it was his twin's doing.

Letting her go only so he could take her face in his hands, he kissed her. He thought he would never stop kissing her, until he heard the earl cough.

Ignoring it the first few times, at last, Philip lifted his head, staring deeply into the tawny eyes of his beloved.

Beryl finally spoke. "Water!"

IN HER COUSIN'S COACH, Beryl sat next to her father, his arm draped around her shoulders, holding her close against his side. She knew she would have to wait until she was home for a drink, since it was only just dawn, and no inn or pub was open.

If only they were at their home in Bedfordshire with the clear waters of the Great Ouse, or even in China where she'd seen rivers and streams of the purest water, she would stop and dunk her head right in. Instead, they rode along beside the filthy Thames, a teasing waterway from which no sane person in London would ever drink, if he or she could help it.

On her other side was Leo, curled in a tight ball, with the curve of his back against her leg. Her little savior!

Across from her, two pairs of eyes stared back, her cousin's and the captain's. The captain who'd already taken her in his arms and kissed her.

She wished she could have brushed her teeth first.

No one seemed eager to talk, everyone perhaps too exhausted.

She could only hope this was her last kidnapping. There was absolutely nothing enjoyable about the experience at all. Except being saved, and even that was losing its luster.

It was Philip who broke the silence, and it wasn't to speak with her. He addressed her father.

"After we drop your daughter home, I intend to head straight to my ship."

Whatever could he mean?

"Are you leaving, Captain?" she ventured to ask.

"No. But there is business to finish to keep you safe."

"As her majesty's representative," her father said, "I believe I should go with you to discuss terms."

Her cousin frowned. "What terms?" Cambrey asked.

"While you were locating Beryl," her father squeezed her shoulder, "Captain Carruthers and I were discussing ways to keep the pirates from trying to take her again. Namely, turning them against . . . ," trailing off, he looked at Philip.

"Chui-A-poo," the captain supplied the name.

"If we can get them to take money and leave, they can say she is dead. I don't really care," Lord Angsley said, "as long as they leave her alone. If they won't agree to help capture Chui-A-poo and turn their leader over to the British in Stanley, then I will ask our queen to capture him or kill him."

"Father!" she said, feeling shocked at his brutality. She'd already seen two dead men in the room through which the pirate had dragged her, and probably, that brute now lay dead in the alley, too.

To think, Leo had wrestled with a pirate. She stroked the cat's head, feeling comforted.

"Lord Angsley is right," Philip said. "Either the queen demands the Qing officials get involved and capture Chui, which is unlikely, or his men do it, which might happen if we pay them enough. Or we'll have to send someone to kill him."

"Probably you," her cousin quipped, and Beryl rested her head back against the leather seat.

Would Philip really go halfway around the world again, on a mission to assassinate a man who had an entire pirate fleet at his disposal?

"I don't like that idea," she said quietly.

No one said anything to that.

Then her father added, "There may already be a return response from the foreign affairs secretary, though unlikely at this hour."

"I'll go, too," her cousin offered.

They all spoke at once, until Cambrey interrupted, "I meant to the captain's ship to meet with the pirates, not to China. Though my wife would strangle me if she knew the adventures I'd already been on tonight."

Then she watched Philip draw something out of his pocket. Holding it out toward her, he dangled her green beryl necklace.

"Oh!" she exclaimed, letting him place it in her hands. It nearly brought her to tears. "After all this time."

"The pirate leader had it," he said quietly.

"Thank you, Captain." She clasped it to her chest, and it brought back memories of the Orient, both bad and exceedingly good.

Staring at him, holding his dark-eyed gaze, she said, "I far prefer my simple necklace to the glittering jewels of the duchess."

Her cousin laughed a tad cynically, but the captain nodded, perhaps in agreement.

And then they were home, and Beryl found herself quickly enveloped in her mother's arms.

A moment later, she saw Lord Wharton. He stood in the open parlor door, looking relieved to see her. It occurred to her a life with him meant no more danger, no more rice sacks over her head. No more dead men.

Thus, when Arthur strode toward her, thanking her father for returning her safely, she allowed him to publicly take her into his arms. Not exactly as the captain had. There was no ardent kiss in front of watchful eyes.

Further, she let him escort her into the parlor and sit beside her on the couch, while he ordered a maid to quickly bring the water she asked for. She expected the other men would follow.

Soon, after drinking it, and then also a glass of her father's brandy, which Arthur pressed into her hand, Beryl realized her cousin and the captain and even her father had all departed without saying goodbye.

Even more belatedly, she wondered what Philip had thought of seeing her fiancé, who'd been comforting and caring—like a nanny, not like a lover.

Reassuring Arthur of her well-being, Beryl at last bid him good day, with the promise of seeing him again soon.

Then, she went upstairs to sink into the hot bath which her maid, who'd been roused early from sleep, drew for her. By the time her hair was washed, too, it was truly dawn, and Beryl was wide awake.

Later, she knew she would probably sleep like the dead, but at that moment, with all the men whom she loved meeting with dangerous pirates, she could only sit with her mother in the parlor and wait.

Rounding the wing chair, she jumped, noticing for the first time that Leo had stayed behind with her and was even then curled up asleep on the blue damask cushion. The shocking realization he was not by his owner's side, looking after the captain, set her heart beating fast. She could only hope the cat knew something she didn't—that he would return uninjured.

PHILIP HAD BEEN PREPARED to hand over the necklace if Beryl's life had depended on it. Now, he wanted Chui's pirates to leave England with a hefty bounty in the hold of their ship and a promise they would dispose of their leader.

And he wanted to forget having seen Beryl wrapped in the arms of her suitable viscount who loved her and whom—Philip assumed—she loved in return.

It was going to take a lot of gin to erase the memory of that reunion.

The Earl of Cambrey thought they should take the direct approach, and simply sit on the deck of the *Robert* and wait. After all, if the pirates even showed up, they already knew their captive had been taken from them and they had nothing to bargain with or for.

Moreover, they were down three men, and Lord Angsley had sent the constable and his police force to remove those bodies.

Philip wondered if they ought to track the rest of Chui's men to their junk at the Limehouse docks rather than let them come on board his ship. In the end, however, agreeing with the earl's assessment, he perched on the same hatch where Beryl had once sat and drunk tea.

Waiting with his new "crew," he kept his revolver on his lap.

All of his old hands had dispersed to their homes, still awaiting payment, which Philip now hoped to have for them within days. And the *Robert* was being prepared for drydock, where she would be made entirely seaworthy once again. For now, she floated gently in the early morning light, tethered in a berth at St. Katharine Docks.

After a few moments, the earl said, "I can see how this is an appealing life."

Philip raised an eyebrow. "Having been aboard for all of ten minutes," he quipped.

All three men laughed.

"Are you going out again soon?" This from Lord Angsley, and Philip couldn't help wondering if the man wanted him gone. Of course, it had been the earl who'd seen him kissing Beryl, not her father, but still, the older gentleman might have an idea.

Then again, maybe not. Maybe they were all simply making polite conversation until this dreadful affair was truly over.

"I have no plans," Philip confessed, wishing he didn't sound shiftless. "My father has a successful wool business, and I might work with him."

"And give up your ship?" Cambrey asked. "I cannot imagine there are a lot of sheep on ships."

No, Philip thought. *Only cats. And where was his loyal moggy?* It hadn't escaped his notice that Leo remained behind in the Angsleys' home. Perhaps the cat had chosen a new owner.

Thinking of Beryl being so brave after all she'd gone through, Philip conceded Leo couldn't have chosen better. And maybe he would bite Lord Wharton—somewhere extremely painful.

"My family's sheep flock and our wool business are in Dumfries," he told the others, "but I confess I prefer our home in Cornwall."

"Ah," the earl mused, "the most pleasant seaside in England."

"Truly, it is," Philip agreed and realized he was happier simply thinking about the small village of Newquay, on the northern Cornish peninsula, overlooking the Bristol Channel.

"The GWR," Lord Angsley mused.

"I beg your pardon?" Philip asked.

"The Great Western Railway," Beryl's father clarified. "It will open up the area, so visitors can come visit your beautiful beaches and take in some healthy sea air."

"I think we already have a Cornwall Railway being built, my lord, though it's on the other side of the peninsula from where my home is."

Lord Angsley shrugged. "I think the GWR will swallow it up in the end. The queen will need a man there who knows what's what to deal with these railway *pirates*."

"I see." *Did he though? Was Angsley offering to help him get a position overseeing rail development in Cornwall?*

Before he could ask more, Chui's men arrived.

Perhaps it was having the able-bodied assistance of the earl and his uncle, but Philip could hardly muster an ounce of fear. Beryl was safe, and the necklace was in his possession again.

"Ahoy," Philip welcomed them, standing as if they were honored guests. There were only two of them, in fact, and so it appeared from the outset as if they knew the jig was up.

After sending skittering glances to each of the men on deck, the pirates bowed low. Philip did the same in return. As he'd discussed with Cambrey and Angsley beforehand, they were to treat these men as equals and with respect in hopes they could be convinced to betray their leader.

"Parley," said one, and Philip nearly laughed at the serious and rather mistaken use of the English pirate term, as if they were in the midst of a battle, with one ship about to be sunk.

"Yes," he agreed. "Captain?" he asked.

The man shook his head and gestured to the one beside him. So, the man who spoke was the translator for the pirate captain. Hopefully, the plan was understandable in very few words.

"You have lost both jewels," Philip began. "The necklace and the woman."

The translator spoke quickly to the captain who looked ill.

"This will mean your death when you again meet Chui-A-poo." Philip waited as words passed between the pirates.

By their expressions, he thought they might end their own lives rather than face Chui.

"Yet it can mean a new life instead." That got their attention.

As simply as he could, he explained the proposal he and Lord Angsley had come up with to keep Beryl safe—capture the pirate leader and turn him over to the British in Stanley. They would, in turn, give him to the Qing government.

There was already a bounty on Chui's head. The pirates would get that, but as incentive, Angsley would give them payment before they even left Britain.

Within a few minutes, the parley was over and the pirates were leaving, certainly happier than when they'd arrived. All they had to do was wait for Angsley to send payment to Limehouse dock, and then they would leave.

Whether it worked or not wouldn't be known for many months.

"It's been a long night," the Earl of Cambrey said. "I, for one, have a wife to get back to."

"As do I," said his uncle.

And just like that, their alliance of necessity was broken, and the titled lords vanished into the sunlight, back to their homes in the most elite and expensive sections of London.

Philip didn't even have a cat anymore.

Nevertheless, bone-deep weary, he went home to his parent's townhouse, a copy of the layout of those in Mayfair simply with a humbler address and fewer floors. After telling his curious siblings about his evening's adventures, he slept longer than he had in months.

The next day, he finally showed his face at Buckingham Palace to present the necklace. He received far more than his agreed-upon reward. Because of Lord Angsley's letter regarding the rescue of his daughter, not to mention the return of the jewels, Philip would be receiving a knighthood.

He couldn't wait to write to Rufus.

Just try to mock me now, Philip thought, truly hoping his good friend would return soon from Scotland. He missed the camaraderie of his likeminded first mate. Those who frequented gentleman's clubs simply would not understand the spirit of the sea which took hold of a man. Once called to it, it was hard to resist, and even more difficult to consider remaining landlocked the rest of one's life. Certainly not as a railway employee!

Whatever else he did, Philip tried to keep his thoughts from Beryl.

That proved harder to do when a day later, she showed up at his doorstep accompanied by her maid and Leo.

CHAPTER FIFTEEN

When told of Miss Beryl Angsley's arrival, Philip bounded down the stairs two at a time, then slowed his pace when his feet hit the foyer floor, not wishing to appear like an eager child.

As he pushed open the drawing room door, Leo nearly tripped him. Dodging between Philip's legs, the cat dashed out of the room, making sure to hiss at him as he passed.

"Hello to you, too," he muttered, actually feeling pleased to see Robert's cat back where he belonged.

And there was Beryl.

He found her in a place he could never have imagined she would be when rescuing her from the junk—seated on his parents' sofa.

"Miss Angsley," Philip greeted, then glanced toward her maid who'd found a discreet seat by his mother's potted ferns. He supposed he wasn't going to be sweeping her into his arms for a kiss.

Beryl rose to her feet, offering him a wry smile, no doubt inwardly laughing at his formality after all they'd been through.

"Captain Carruthers," she returned in equal formality, holding out her hand so he had to come to her.

Bending his head over her gloved hand, he refrained from kissing it. She was engaged, he reminded himself.

"To what do I owe this pleasure?"

She tilted her head, taking her measure of him, giving him a moment to do the same. She looked damnably well. Refreshed, glossy hair with not a grain of rice in sight, and a gown so lovely and well-fitted, it made him wonder what she could possibly wear to dress up for an important occasion.

"I simply thought you might be missing Leo, and he, you," she said at last.

He grinned. "Yes, I could see how much he missed me as he ran by."

"At our home, he was likely to get sat upon or tripped over. I have five siblings, you may recall. Some very young still."

"I believe I saw one or two of them the night of your kidnapping." He recalled crying children in the hallway and on the stairs.

"My *second* kidnapping," she corrected with a grimace.

"Hopefully your last."

"Dear God, yes! I have no desire ever to set foot on a ship again. At least, not one going to the Orient."

Inside, he felt a little sheen of optimism evaporate. How ridiculous he had still thought she might want to sail away with him to ports unknown. It was no life for a lady. Hell, it was hardly a life for him!

"Completely understandable," he agreed, even though, with the lack of anything interesting to do here in England, he was certain he would set sail as soon as an opportunity arose. It was either that or learn to sheer sheep.

"Thank you for returning him. When I do launch the *Robert* again, I believe Leo will want to be aboard. She's currently in drydock undergoing a few repairs."

Beryl nodded. "So, you are sailing away again?"

"Indubitably," he said. *Why did she ask? Did she wish him to stay? If she did and if she wasn't getting married—*

"That's the best thing for you," she said, interrupting his fantasies.

"Yes."

They stared at one another.

"I shouldn't have kissed you in the alley," Philip blurted.

Her eyes widened, and she glanced over her shoulder at her maid. It was probably the most exciting thing the girl had heard in hours. Perhaps Beryl didn't recall her cousin had been standing there at the time, as well.

For his part, he had kissed her as if he'd had a right to display his relief and his affection, and it had given him false hope she could be his for the taking.

She was already taken.

And she'd been in a state of shock, making his kiss even less appropriate. He'd taken advantage of her.

"It was not the gentlemanly thing to do," he clarified.

"True, Captain, but I never thought of you as a gentleman."

That hurt, and his expression must have shown it.

"Oh, dear," she said. "That came out entirely wrong.

BERYL INWARDLY CURSED HERSELF for her own stupidity.

"What I meant to say is, when I think of you, if I were to think of you, not that I am, of course, but if I do, at all, I think of you as a man of adventure. Not a pirate, certainly, not after seeing real pirates, but as a sea captain ready for daring actions, like Odysseus, himself, whose story I was reading in your cabin."

"Deeds of derring-do," Philip muttered.

"Precisely," she agreed, hoping he was not offended, for she had meant no offense. Quite the contrary, she much preferred his behavior to any man she knew. Even Arthur, though he had been the very embodiment of gentlemanly concern for days now.

Cloying, suffocating, gentlemanly concern. It was only his dislike of cats that had stopped him accompanying her today. He couldn't bear to be confined in a carriage with one.

"Slinky, evil animal!" he'd declared when he first found Leo seated beside her on the couch. And he'd shooed him off and out of the parlor.

She supposed, after they got married, she would get a dog, for she quite liked having a companion.

"I'm glad we had a better outcome than that of Odysseus," the captain reminded her. "He was away from home twenty years as I recall."

"It wasn't all unpleasant," she mused. "He had Kalypso." Instantly, her thoughts turned to descriptions of the goddess luring the captain to her secluded grotto and her bed, and her cheeks heated.

Philip's eyes seemed to darken, if that were possible. She'd seen it before, each time before he reached for her and pulled her close.

Would he do so now?

After his kiss in the alley, Beryl had waited for him each night, hoping he would scale her home again, however he'd managed it, and sneak into her room. She wanted to revisit the sensations she'd experienced under his touch. Moreover, she wanted to return them, causing him to feel the same pleasure. And, dammit, she wanted to be kissed so her whole body caught fire.

She'd waited in vain, half hoping he was going to declare for her, perhaps even ask her father, who seemed to admire Captain Carruthers, for permission to engender a proposal. Alas, he hadn't.

Thus, she'd come to him, with the flimsy excuse of returning Leo, who'd seemed perfectly happy, except for Arthur scooting him constantly out of the way with the toe of his Hessian boot.

Moreover, she'd worn one of her favorite peach-pink gowns. Still, all Philip had done was apologize for the last time he kissed her.

As if it had been a mistake instead of an act of passion. Maybe even of love?

"Kalypso was a diversion," the captain pointed out. "A magical time, but one that could only happen while away from home. Odysseus had Penelope, his true love, waiting for him."

He paused and added, "As you had Lord Wharton."

She swallowed. *So now she was Odysseus, Philip was Kalypso, and Arthur was the long-suffering Penelope?*

Thinking about it that way made her head—and heart—hurt. For it seemed Captain Carruthers, as Kalypso with Odysseus, had decided to let her go to get on with her ordinary, commonplace, humdrum life in England.

There was nothing she could do about that. If he wanted her for himself, he could certainly have her, and she thought by her actions in her bedroom and by allowing his kiss in the alley, she had made that fact abundantly clear.

She could not, however, compete with the lure of a free and exciting life at sea. At least he respected her enough not to try to turn her into his Jenny with a cracked teacup—*was that what he'd called women in port all those months ago in practically their first conversation?* Whatever he'd been talking about, she was certain it didn't apply to ladies of her class.

"I must be going," she said, suddenly realizing the futility of her mission. Also, it smacked of desperation, which was the opposite of how she wanted to portray herself. Besides, she wasn't desperate. She had a perfectly good fiancé, as she kept reminding herself.

Philip frowned. "Forgive my manners. We've spent the entire time standing, and I didn't even offer you tea."

"No, but I came to give you Leo, and I have done so."

He nodded. "Very well. I thank you for my cat. What's more, I'm glad to see you are well and didn't sustain any injuries during either of your abductions."

"Thanks to you." Even if he didn't want her, cracked or not, she owed him her life and would always be grateful.

Nodding to her maid to follow, Beryl let the captain escort her to the front door. Turning in the foyer, she noticed Leo was sitting halfway up the stairs, and her fingers itched to go to him and give him a last pet. She resisted.

"I suppose I may never see you again," she said to him, feeling as if she might choke on the emotion her own words caused to well in her throat.

He shook his head, a small smile crossing his handsome face.

"Don't be ridiculous, Miss Angsley. I have saved your life, which means I am responsible for it forever."

"Does it?" That cheered her more than a little. "So, if I'm ever in need of you—"

"I'll be at your service, Miss Angsley."

She was still pondering their encounter a few days later when an envelope came from Buckingham Palace addressed to her!

Upon opening it, her heart began to quicken its pace.

"Father," she yelled as she hurried through the house, behaving more like one of her younger sisters or brothers.

"Yes, dear daughter?" he asked, rising from his desk in alarm.

"We are going to Westminster Abbey to watch Captain Carruthers get his knighthood!"

FOR THE NEXT TWO weeks, Beryl could hardly contain her excitement. That she had played a part in Captain Carruthers being invested with a knighthood was quite astounding. True, all she'd done was get herself kidnapped and he'd done the rest, but still, it wouldn't be happening without her.

What's more, it gave her an excuse to see him again.

What's more, because of their gratitude, her parents were coming, and because of his love for her, Lord Wharton was coming. Or was it because he'd never been close to the queen and kept saying what an honor it would be?

"I would think the biggest honor would be thanking Captain Carruthers for saving my life," Beryl pointed out, even though she couldn't really fault Arthur for his excitement. After all, Queen Victoria was the most beloved monarch anyone could recall.

It took Beryl and her mother a week to decide on their clothing. Another week to change their minds and then a few days more to consider their hairstyles.

In the end, none of it mattered, for all eyes were on the queen wearing the mantle and insignia of the order of knighthood she'd chosen for the captain, as well as on her dashing prince consort. And when not staring at them in all their regal magnificence, everyone's eyes were drawn to the abbey, itself, as they strolled along the nave, with its soaring, uplifting ceiling, seeming to reach Heaven.

Beryl knew she could be wearing the hated rice sack and no one would notice. Which was as it should be. As for the captain, he looked every inch a knight-errant as the queen tapped his shoulder with a sword and declared him to be a Knight Grand Cross of the Most Honourable Order of the Bath.

At which point, Beryl heard the red-headed Scot seated nearby, whom she recognized as the first mate of the *Robert*, repeat the words "Order of the Bath" with a decidedly sardonic tone.

Arthur leaned close and whispered, "They used to purify the knight in a bath and put him to bed to dry."

He said it so seriously while uttering such comical words, Beryl had to clamp her hand to her mouth to keep from laughing. Unfortunately, Philip glanced her way at that moment, and she hoped he didn't think she found him humorous. She most certainly didn't. She thought he looked more striking and had more dash-fire than anyone else there, including Prince Albert and all the other knights who'd congregated for the investiture.

Then the prince consort pinned the insignia on Philip's robes, before moving down the line of two other men also receiving the honor that day.

Before Beryl knew it, it was over, and they were outside in the watery sunshine. It was only then she saw Leo, slipping out through the abbey's massive west doors when someone conveniently opened them, traipsing lightly on his paws toward where they were gathered.

For the second time that day, she wanted to laugh heartily.

"You seem very amused by my knighthood, Miss Angsley," Philip said, his first utterance of the day said directly to her.

"Oh, Captain, I mean *Sir* Carruthers," she corrected herself, watching him blush slightly, "it is not your knighthood that amused me, I promise. I think it well-earned and am honored to be here. But only see who was in the abbey watching."

And she gestured to where Leo stood on his stocky legs observing their group.

Rufus, who stood with Mr. Churley, started to laugh in earnest.

"From what I hear," he said, "the bloody cat should've received a knighthood as well."

They all chuckled, except Arthur, who griped, "I think the animal rather lowers the solemnity of the occasion." And he sniffed.

Beryl rolled her eyes, feeling a little embarrassed by the man she would soon marry, a mere few weeks away now.

The captain—for even though he was now a knight, she would always think of him thusly—ignored Arthur. Turning to his proud parents standing beside him, he remarked, "I think Robert sent the cat in his place today."

His mother teared up and his father shook his hand. His two delightful siblings whom Beryl had only just met, both a few years younger than herself, hugged their brother.

Beryl's heart ached thinking this might be the last time she was in the captain's presence. More than anything, she wished she could put her arms around him, draw his head down to hers, and kiss him.

Of course, she couldn't do anything of the kind. For the next time she was in the house of God, it would be on her wedding day.

CHAPTER SIXTEEN

That night, carousing with Rufus and Churley in a god-awful gin palace, Philip couldn't keep his thoughts off of Beryl. She'd been breathtaking in her purple silk gown, and he'd wanted to stand up before his queen, her parents—and her goddamned fiancé—and declare his love for her. She was funny, brave, intelligent, and lovely.

With each glass of gin, his mood plummeted. He had to leave her to her planned, expected life, filled with luxury and all the social graces she deserved—along with marriage to a peer of the realm.

And he certainly wasn't going to attend, even though he'd been invited, right there on the steps of Westminster Abbey.

"Of course, we're so grateful for her safe return," Lord Wharton had said, "you simply must share our happy day to see the future you've allowed to happen."

Philip had tried to exchange a glance with Beryl to see her thoughts on her upcoming wedding, but she was staring at her husband-to-be.

In the end, he had muttered something noncommittal, rather than the "Hell fire but no!" that he was thinking.

Then Beryl had asked him what he was planning to do next, another mission for the queen, perhaps.

Again, he'd been vague because he really didn't know.

"I may be going back to sea or even up to Dumfries." Then he'd looked at his father for a sign of his destiny. "I have no desire at present for a long voyage," he'd added, though if Beryl asked him to go for merely enough silk to make the gown she was wearing, Philip would drop everything and sail around the world for her.

What a lovestruck fool!

Beryl had made a sound of agreement. "I, for one, am determined never to return to the Orient."

"No," Arthur agreed. "A dreadful place, obviously."

This time, Philip had caught her gaze and held it. *Was she thinking about the not dreadful and very wonderful things that had happened, like their first kiss, their long talks, more kisses?*

"Not that you asked me to," she'd added, her eyes still on his.

"No," he'd replied, speaking to her alone, thinking of her safety as the utmost important thing in his life. "I wouldn't."

Then, as everyone was staring at him, he'd added, "The sea is no place for a woman."

Rufus had barked out a laugh. "Tell that to Ching Shih." And then he'd told the others of the Chinese pirate lady who'd ruled the seas around the Orient and beyond for many years.

"Fascinating," Beryl's mother had said. "To think of a woman with such power."

At that moment, Queen Victoria, surrounded by her guards left the abbey, and they all stared wide-eyed.

"Not so unusual after all," Lord Angsley pointed out. "Congratulations, again, *Sir* Carruthers."

He'd winced. "I think I'll remain *captain*, thank you, or even *mister.*"

"Or Lord C—" Rufus had begun.

"Don't say it," Philip had cut him off.

The group had disbanded, and for a moment, Philip watched as Beryl strolled away on Lord Wharton's arm, walking into her future as the man had said.

"Let's go get ran-tan immediately. And nowhere fancy either."

"Aye, aye, Captain," Rufus and Churley had agreed.

Thus, they now found themselves drunk and happy, or at least drunk, and surrounded by gin-scented whores.

As his first mate and his quartermaster decided upon which women they would tup, Philip quietly staggered out into the night.

There was Leo!

"You're going to get kidnapped or run over one day if you're not careful."

Instantly terrified at the idea of losing Robert's cat, Philip did something he never did. He scooped him up into his arms.

"Now, now," he soothed as Leo hissed and yowled. He squeezed him close in a manly hug.

Struggling, letting Leo give him a few good scratches, Philip held onto him for blocks until he found his carriage, and then he let him leap from his arms to the seat. It was not the fancy clarence of his father, suitable for transporting ladies. Nor was it a dangerous top-heavy phaeton, such as his brother had raced and died in

It was simply a lightweight tilbury. Perfect for a bachelor and his cat. Though he supposed, if he had a lady friend, a covered interior suitable for trysts would be desirable. Instead, uncovered, he faced the London elements of soot and fog and headed home—a newly invested knight of the realm.

"STUPID, STUPID, STUPID!" BERYL said aloud.

"Stop it," Eleanor told her. "You are not stupid."

"But I was content before and now I feel restless. I should never have gone with my father."

Eleanor wrinkled her nose. "Really? You would have missed out on the adventure of a lifetime in order to feel content?"

It was not the lack of adventure in her life. It was the lack of Philip Carruthers. However, she couldn't tell her friend that. If she spoke it, it would be a terrible betrayal to Arthur. Besides, Philip had disappeared after the investiture ceremony, and she'd never heard from him again. It felt like months though it had been merely a couple weeks. It might as well be years, for she had no reason to think she would ever see him again. *Not ever!*

If she had never journeyed to the Orient and never met him, she would, indeed, be content and looking forward to married life as the biggest adventure she could imagine. Instead, the closer she came to her wedding day, the more unsettled she became.

At that moment, seated in the drawing room with Eleanor, she simply wanted the ceremony over so she didn't have to think of possible, yet unrealistic, alternatives any longer. As soon as she was Lady Wharton, she could begin to run her own household. Then her next adventure would be motherhood.

"I'm going to be a mother," she said softly.

"What?" Eleanor jumped up. "Have you and Arthur—?"

"No!" Beryl interrupted her friend from even saying the words. *Why, they'd barely kissed.*

"I'm sorry, sit down. I'm only thinking of the future. My mind is racing. Let's go back to discussing the wedding breakfast, shall we?"

"Did you decide where to go after the nuptials? You are taking a honeymoon, aren't you?"

Beryl nodded. "I would like to go to Land's End."

"To Cornwall?" Eleanor frowned. "It is very far and deserted."

"True, but people say it is lovely—the beaches, the coves, the pirate lodgings."

"Pirates?" Eleanor exclaimed

"What?" Beryl jumped at the word.

Her friend sipped her lemonade and frowned. "You said *pirate* lodgings."

"No, I said *private* lodgings. Or at least, I meant to. Anyway, I doubt we shall go. Arthur wishes to take a boat from the Old Swan Pier across the river to Gravesend and spend a day there."

Eleanor wrinkled her nose. "That's not much of a wedding trip."

"Agreed. It's all cockle-boats and ugly piers and not enough soft sand or pretty ocean. You remember last time you and I went. It was so crowded."

"And the shrimp," Eleanor reminded her.

They laughed at the memory. "True, everywhere, those awful signs: 'Tea and shrimps, ninepence.' I hardly think they go together. Plus, why would one ever spend the night there?"

"Certainly not your wedding night. Cornwall does sound better. Rather romantic, in fact."

"Yes," Beryl agreed. The idea of drifting off to sleep with the ocean lapping at the land, enclosed in Philip's arms, as he told her stories of the pirates of Perranporth—absolutely heavenly.

Arthur's arms. Dammit!

"If I push for a seaside honeymoon, we shall probably end up at Ramsgate or Dover. So much closer. And Arthur is not one for travelling far."

They both sipped their drinks in silence. Arthur and she would have to suit one another. They simply must. After all, hadn't she said she'd had enough adventure for a lifetime?

STRANGE HOW PHILIP COULDN'T focus upon his father's words whenever they discussed the wool business or going up to Dumfries to visit their sheep flocks.

Suddenly, he realized his father had paused and was perhaps awaiting a response.

"Yes," Philip said into the silence.

"Yes?" Douglas Carruthers looked confused.

"Uh, no?" he tried again. "Emphatically, no."

His father sighed. "Never you mind." Pushing his chair back, he stood. "You haven't been listening to a word I've said. I could talk till I'm blue in the face and I would never get you interested in shearing and combing or, God forbid, moth grubs. Why, you don't even know the difference between woolen and worsted fabrics."

"True," Philip said with a shrug. "I could learn."

His father shook his head but without a trace of disappointment.

"You will never concentrate on sheep long enough to learn. No matter how lucrative. But then, I couldn't figure out one sail from another or how to tie a sailor's knot to save my life. That was always your mother's people."

Philip nodded in agreement. His father had let his family enjoy their summers in Cornwall by the sea, but he'd never entered the water as far as Philip could remember. Nor had Douglas Carruthers been able to assist his twin sons in building their small boats and sailing them just beyond the waves.

"I suppose I'll join the ranks of the merchant seaman."

"Not the navy?" his father asked, then offered a smile to match his son's. Plainly, neither of them could picture it.

"Afraid not, Father. Too many orders from people who have no business giving them. I don't wish to end up in one of Britain's colonial sea battles, either, sent to Davy Jones's locker over sugarcane or slaves."

His father put a hand on his shoulder. "And I don't want to lose another fine son."

Philip caught his breath. It was the kindest words his father had said since losing Robert.

"Besides, you're a knight now, there must be some way to turn that into a living."

Philip chuckled. "I'll see if someone at the palace will pay me to ride around the country rescuing damsels and being chivalrous."

They both laughed.

"Actually, the queen's foreign secretary sent a letter indicating there is some mission coming up." Philip had been surprised to get the official letter, even more so when he was told Lord Angsley would be contacting him next.

"As long as you're not away so long next time," his father said. "Hard on your mother, that was."

When his father left him alone, sitting in the back garden of their townhouse, he kept thinking of damsels in distress, at least one, anyway. And even though he ought to make a decision about his life, he had to wait and find out what Lord Angsley had to do with it.

"GLAD TO SEE YOU, Captain."

"And you, sir." Philip was finally back at Beryl's home, summoned there by her father, and he could only hope for a glimpse of her.

"Sorry for the delay. It's been rather busy around here what with my getting a new post and my daughter's wedding preparations. More to do to get married these days than preparing for the Battle of Waterloo, I'd warrant."

Philip's heart sank. Why he'd let himself imagine Lord Angsley needing to speak with him had anything to do with Beryl's wedding—particularly it being called off—Philip couldn't fathom his own foolishness.

"I wouldn't know, my lord."

"Dresses, more than one, food and flowers, and music and guests. All far too much import placed upon the day rather than on what follows."

"My lord?" Her father could *not* mean the wedding night, though that was all Philip could think of—Lord Arthur pasty-face Wharton taking his new bride to bed.

Realizing his hands had become fists, he relaxed and focused on the man seated opposite him.

"Yes," Lord Angsley continued, "I mean, the many years of marriage are what matter, not the blasted ceremony or the wedding breakfast, which seems to be growing into a wedding feast of epic proportions."

What could Philip say? Absolutely nothing. Years of waking up next to Beryl as his wife and going to sleep after making love to her seemed like a very good idea.

"You didn't ask me, Captain."

Philip frowned.

"About my new post I just mentioned. Your thoughts were all for the wedding, I suppose as everyone else's around here. Do you wish to attend? Only fitting, I suppose, seeing as how there wouldn't be a wedding without you."

"No," Philip said, then realized he'd practically shouted. "I mean, I'm sure it's a family event. Please, my lord, tell me of your new post." For one more word about Beryl getting married, and he was going to lose his sanity.

"I've been made the Royal Diplomatic Envoy to Spain, removed from the Far East route, thank God and thank the queen!"

Philip wasn't sure how to respond. "That's good news if you're happy with the appointment."

"Oh, definitely. Makes life easier all the way around. Only think how close it is. Nice climate, too. I consider it a reward for my time served in the Orient."

"It sounds like an honor, my lord," he offered, still wondering why the man felt he had to confide in him.

"I'm not sure about an honor, Captain. It's not akin to your knighthood. In fact, you'll notice a large number of barons and viscounts in the diplomatic ranks. There are so many of us, we are expendable," he joked. "Not like your rare marquess or duke."

"I see." Philip had never thought about it before, and to agree seemed an insult.

"To get to the point, I'll need a ship to take me to the sunny shores of the Iberian Peninsula. I told the queen yours would be quite suitable."

The words filtered through his foggy brain, distracted by weddings and barons, like sunshine cutting through clouds.

"*My* ship? You wish to use the *Robert* as an ambassador's transport."

"Exactly! Unlike going to the Orient, I can't show up in the Mediterranean Sea in a Royal Naval warship now, can I? Things are too shaky in that part of the world, and we'd be at war before you know it. With their leadership always changing and their civil wars and coups, I'll need to go through the Straits of Gibraltar about once a month. Are you game for such a mission, Captain?"

Without hesitation, Philip answered, "Yes, my lord. I am."

"First, you'll need to build me a comfortable cabin. Unless you want me to confiscate yours."

"No, my lord. I don't," he said frankly and, hopefully, without affront.

Lord Angsley laughed. "Naturally, the crown will pay for any renovations. Also, we may host a foreign dignitary on board from time to time, so we need a stateroom that looks . . . well, stately."

"Of course." Philip's brain was rushing ahead as to where they could fit in a stateroom worthy of the British monarch's representative. Moreover, would his cook's fare be suitable? *What a wonderful dilemma!*

"You look, if I may say, Captain, a good deal happier than you did when you entered my office. And I haven't even told you about your compensation yet."

Then the door opened behind him, and the hair on the back of Philip's neck stood on end. Without turning, even before he heard her gasp in surprise, he knew it was Beryl.

CHAPTER SEVENTEEN

Standing, as did her father, Philip felt his heartbeat quicken at the sight of her. Beryl looked more beautiful, if possible, every time he laid eyes upon her. Or maybe, he was simply fonder of her each time.

She had stopped in the doorway, soft brown eyes wide, lips slightly parted. If her father hadn't been in the room, she would be in his arms already.

"I do apologize," she began, her gaze fixed on his. "I had no idea you had company, Father."

"Quite all right," Lord Angsley said. "You remember the captain, I'm sure. We had just concluded our business."

Realizing he hadn't yet said a word, Philip greeted her. "It's good to see you, Miss Angsley."

"Thank you, Captain. I hope you are well."

"I am, thank you. And you?" He wanted to scream at the inanity of polite conversation.

"I am."

They had used up all the frivolous welcome words. *Now what?*

"Beryl, did you need me?" her father asked.

"Why, yes, I . . . ," she trailed off, looking down at the cloth in her hands. Her cheeks pinkened. "I wanted to know which color waistcoat you wished the tailor to use."

Philip saw she was holding two different swatches of fine brocade.

"Oh," Lord Angsley said, "more wedding day decisions. Honestly, dear girl, I don't mind. Whatever you and your mother think is best."

Beryl nodded, and Philip felt as though the walls were closing in. The room seemed smaller than his cabin privy and with half as much air. He needed to get out of there.

"I'm sure the captain doesn't want his time wasted on such matters," his lordship said.

"No, my lord," Philip agreed. Then hoping that wasn't rude, he added, "I am certain whatever you choose, Miss Angsley, it will be the best. I must take my leave."

Except she was blocking his exit.

"Please walk our guest out," Lord Angsley said to his daughter, causing Beryl's cheeks to turn redder.

Philip turned back to her father and they shook hands on their new arrangement.

"You'd best get started on those renovations, Captain."

"I will, my lord." With a small bow, he took his leave, finding himself walking behind the shapely figure who haunted his nights.

In the foyer, she asked, "What renovations is my father referring to?"

"To the *Robert*. I'll be getting her ready for diplomatic use."

Her eyes lit with interest. "For my father?"

"Precisely."

She nodded her approval. "My mother is very pleased about his new post."

At that moment, three of her siblings ran down the stairs, through the foyer, and along the hall to the back of the house. The third in line stuck his tongue out at Beryl on his way.

Philip laughed. "I can see why she might not want Lord Angsley so far away for a year at a time."

"Precisely," Beryl mimicked his word.

They stared at one another.

"Perhaps when I am settled," she said, "I will take my siblings for a few weeks and let my mother travel with my father."

When she was settled, meaning married. Philip hated to think of that day.

"What will your husband," he asked, nearly choking on the word, "say to that?"

She shrugged slightly. "Arthur is quite amenable actually. He likes my brothers and sisters."

Undoubtedly, he also rescued puppies and was in line for a sainthood.

"Perhaps when you are settled," Philip considered, "then you will wish to take a trip with your father again."

Her eyes opened wide at the thought, and then, *dammit*, her gaze went to his mouth, and he knew what she was thinking. If they were in close confines of his ship for any length of time, they would end up in a passionate embrace.

"No," she said after a pause. "That would not be possible. Even if you can create one stateroom for my father, I don't believe you have room to build another one."

As if that were the issue.

"I would give you my bed," he said, his voice unintentionally turning husky. "I mean, my entire cabin, of course."

Beryl stared down at the fabric in her arms. Material for her wedding dress. When she looked up at him again, the softness of her expression had vanished. She looked determined, focused, even obstinate.

"No, Captain. I think not. When I am a happily married viscountess, I'll have many duties keeping me here safely on shore. Speaking of duties, I must get back to them."

She nodded to the Angsley butler, standing quietly by, and he opened the door wide.

Leo sat on the step, washing his paws in the midday sun. Looking up as the door opened, his paw halfway to his mouth, his tongue out, he was the picture of feline adorableness.

Predictably, Beryl cooed in delight. "Leo! Why on earth didn't he come in?"

Philip shook his head. She said it as if he were an honored guest and not a mangy orange-yellow moggy.

Thrusting the bolts of brocade into Philip's arms, Beryl bent down and scooped up the cat. Philip could swear the cat yelped in surprise. Allowing himself to be stroked was one thing, even snuggling beside her on the bed in the ship's cabin—*who wouldn't want to?*—but being unceremoniously picked up and held like a baby was quite another. *Would Leo stand for it?*

Ready in case he had to knock the beast out of her arms if he tried to scratch her, Philip watched as she rubbed her chin on Leo's soft head, and then, to his amazement, he heard the loud purring begin.

The cat was entirely in love with Miss Beryl Angsley. Just as he was. He should toss the stupid cloth to the floor, take her in his arms, and offer her a life of . . . *what exactly?*

A room in his parents' townhouse and a cramped ship's cabin. She was rather clear in looking forward to her life as a viscount's wife. How could he hope to match the luxuries and the social opportunities that accompanied such a title? He couldn't.

"I will leave you to your wedding plans," he said, knowing he sounded stiff.

The door was already open after all, but should he take his cat from her arms and risk death by feline or ask her to put Leo down?

Deciding on the latter, he stepped outside.

"Captain," her tone sounded expectant, as she lowered Leo to his paws on the stoop beside him.

"Yes." Whatever she asked of him, he would do.

"Will you attend my wedding?"

Except that!

"No, thank you, Miss Angsley. I have no interest in weddings, neither ceremonies nor feasts." And he gave the waistcoat fabric back to her. "Good day."

He turned quickly so he didn't have to look at the disappointment in her eyes.

IT WAS HER WEDDING day, at last. Arthur had surprised her with a beautiful bracelet the night before, and now Beryl was holding still as her maid fastened it to her wrist. Diamonds and sapphires, nothing from the beryl family of gemstones, but he wasn't to know that even mattered.

In a few hours, she would be newly titled Lady Wharton. *Nice.*

It was as strong an emotion as she could summon. She wasn't terribly unhappy about it. He was a caring man, and after a few tries, she'd taught him how to slant his head so their mouths fit well, but so far, she couldn't quite get herself to touch his tongue, and he hadn't tried to thrust his into her mouth, either.

That would come later, perhaps tonight. She wasn't even too bothered about getting undressed in front of him, so utterly comfortable with him, as if he were her favorite dressing gown or house slippers.

Assuredly, she told herself, it was better than always having butterflies take flight in one's stomach upon seeing a certain captain. Or having one's cheeks heat up and one's mouth go dry. Occasionally, she'd even experienced shortness of breath around Philip Carruthers. None of that could be healthy. Nor should it be the least bit desirable.

It wasn't. She was very fond of Arthur, and they would suit.

Besides, Philip had said he had no interest in weddings, and she assumed he meant his own, as well. Truly, he didn't seem the type of man to go to work in an office and then come home in the evening, day in day out. He seemed the type of man best suited to standing behind the wheel with the wind in his beautiful dark hair.

Staring into the looking glass, wearing a gown in the palest blue so it was nearly white, she wondered what the captain would think of—

No! She wondered what *Arthur* would think of it.

"Are we finished?" Beryl snapped at her maid, instantly regretting the peevish tone to her voice. "What I mean, Emma, is you have done such a lovely job with my hair and dress, I cannot imagine there's anything else to do."

"Yes, miss. I believe your parents are ready to leave."

Good. She wanted to get this day over with and get on with her life. As soon as the ceremony was over, the registry signed, and they left the vestry, they would hold the bridal breakfast at her cousin's home since the Earl of Cambrey had a larger entertaining room at Cavendish Square than they had at her own home. The many presents had all be taken there and put on display in the Cambreys' drawing room. Even Beryl's travelling suit was already there, laid out in a guest bedroom for her to don after the celebratory meal.

Her trunk was packed for a week's long trip to the seaside. Arthur had said if they had to go farther than Gravesend, then he avowed it would not be to Ramsgate. Though good enough for Queen Victoria when she was a child, the seaside town was now considered a bit shabby. Instead, they had two tickets on the South Eastern Railway to Dover, where they would see the chalky cliffs and enjoy the new pier, ice rink, and bathing machines, and stay in a lovely hotel room on the main crescent.

Nice.

Soon, Beryl arrived at the church, All Souls on Regent Street, holding flowers in her hands, the palms of which were inexplicably moist. Why she was even the littlest bit anxious, she couldn't fathom. Everything was in order—the church having been correctly named in the license and both she and Arthur living within its parish. Her fiancé had even insisted on the banns being published on three successive Sundays by the officiating clergymen, though with the regular license, it was unnecessary.

The sandy-colored stone building designed by the famed architect John Nash was both a little strange and also quite beautiful. Entering beneath the oft-ridiculed, overly pointy spire—which made Beryl think of a medieval lance—she passed between the expansive Corinthian columns with her family and into the vestibule.

As she crossed the gray and green mosaic-tiled foyer in her wedding slippers, she could hear voices of family and friends floating out from the church's interior.

This is it, she thought.

As she followed her bridesmaids, including Eleanor, down the main aisle of the nave toward her fiancé and his groomsmen, Beryl stopped counting pews after fourteen. She ought to be thinking deep and loving thoughts about God and Arthur Wharton, not counting the seats. *What was wrong with her?*

Her heartbeat seemed to quicken the closer she got to the altar and the rector smiling benignly at her. Glancing up at the soaring ceiling, trying to think peaceful thoughts, she took in the second story of each of the side aisles, and their symmetrical line of columns, giving the entire church a lofty and classical feel. The upstairs pews were empty as her father had kept the guest list down to a manageable hundred or so.

She was glad at that moment not to have more eyes peering down at her, perhaps judging her. For she was feeling a little fraudulent, having discussed with Eleanor earlier in the morning how tepid her and Arthur's emotions truly were.

Eleanor had told her to call off the whole thing.

Beryl had laughed at that. Now, she didn't feel like laughing. Instead, she reminded herself there were brides all over Britain who'd married with only fond feelings and had long and happy marriages.

Or so she supposed.

The sole thought that niggled at her, ate at her with every step she took toward saying her vows with Arthur, was this: *I love Philip Carruthers with my entire heart and soul.*

CHAPTER EIGHTEEN

Philip was pacing along the length of his empty ship, from the fo'c'sle to the main deck to the quarter deck to the poop deck, and back again. Rufus had been there the night before, listening to Philip's drunken ranting over the uselessness of viscounts.

"Then take the lass for yourself, dammit!" Rufus had said finally. "You'll never be happy elsewise, and I'm bloody sick of listening to you." Then he'd left.

Leo was not pacing with him. He was sitting on the railing with his back to the ship looking toward the Thames. The cat hadn't looked the least upset when Philip had awakened moaning with a splitting headache after only a couple hours of sleep, nor had he looked concerned when his owner wretched over the side onto the ground below for his ship was still in drydock. It would remain there for another week. No longer needing repairs, the *Robert* was nearly finished being refitted for the use of Her Majesty's royal emissary to Spain.

Except Philip didn't think he could do it. How could he sail with Beryl's father, with the man being a constant reminder of the woman he loved? Undoubtedly, Lord

Angsley would tell him how she fared in her married life, thinking Philip would want to hear her latest news after saving her life.

One day, her father would undoubtedly tell him of her being with child. Philip had decided he could pretend Beryl and pasty-faced Arthur had no conjugal relations until that moment. Then, he could imagine tossing himself into the sea.

"Get yourself together, man!" Philip snarled, and Leo's head whipped around, locking his thoughtful yellow eyes with his owner's.

Was the cat telling him something? Slowly, Leo leaped from the railing, slunk low to the deck, and pounced past him.

When next the cat approached him, he had a mouse slung from his jaws. Quite dead.

Philip slapped his forehead with his palm at his own foolishness, then groaned in pain from the headache. *A message from the cat! What an idiot!*

But, on second thought, maybe it was. Leo knew what he wanted and he took it—like a true pirate—though the mouse might not appreciate his determination. The cat also had bestowed his affections carefully, purposefully it seemed, on one particular lady. A lady so worthy of love, Philip couldn't imagine ever feeling the same about another, no matter how he tried.

Moreover, he didn't want to try. He wanted Beryl.

If he thought she had no inclination toward him in return, Philip hoped he would be civil enough to ignore his own and to leave her be. Yet she had melted in his arms, and he'd known the desire to please her for the rest of their lives. And he still hadn't even tupped her yet!

Glancing around his ship, he decided it was as good a home as any. His cabin had been spruced up while the other repairs had been made. Moreover, his mother had already given him the house in Newquay, with the most beautiful views and peaceful harbor, a perfect place to take their ease when they were in England. Indeed, a perfect place to raise children.

Unless Beryl truly wanted the life of a viscountess and desired London's social whirl.

"I far prefer my simple necklace to the glittering jewels of the duchess," she'd said in the coach, staring into his eyes after her second rescue.

Only one woman in a thousand would say such. *Perhaps a woman who didn't mind being a sea captain's wife instead of a viscount's.*

Philip felt it begin in his toes and work its way up his body, an uncivilized, lawless—even barbaric—sensation. A resolve to take what he wanted.

"I am a bloody pirate," he yelled, with only the cat to hear.

It was still early, thank God, too early for the wedding to have taken place. Maybe he had two hours if he was lucky.

Disembarking down the plank that rested against the side of his ship, he'd hailed a hackney within minutes. First, he would head home to wash and change, and then stop at Rufus's house, for he needed help to carry out his ill-conceived, rash plan. His piratical plan.

Then the two of them—three, he amended, as Leo sat beside him—would race to the church of All Souls, where her father had told him the wedding would take place.

BERYL HANDED HER BOUQUET to Eleanor and let Arthur take hold of her hands. If only she could stop them trembling!

The rector was saying something, but her ears were buzzing and she couldn't understand his words. In her own head, she could hear herself saying something she definitely should not say out loud, "I cannot marry you, Arthur."

Biting her lip to keep from blurting out the thought that would ruin this lovely day, offend her fiancé, insult his family, disrupt the wedding, inconvenience the guests, and possibly disappoint her parents, she nearly drew blood.

Then a murmur began at the front of the church, and she glanced back along the nave.

Leo! He was sauntering up the main aisle, looking right and left as people made sounds or laughed. Some tried to get him to stop, with "Puss, puss, come here," but he kept walking until he came to a halt directly in front of her, gazing up with those gorgeous golden eyes.

A laugh, admittedly nervous, bordering on hysterical, erupted from Beryl's throat.

"I don't think this is funny at all," Arthur protested. "In fact, it's disgusting. A flea-bitten animal, here, in church."

The rector made a choking sound. "Actually, there is quite a long history of animals being blessed. St. Francis, for instance—"

"Vicar, please!" Arthur said to stop the man giving a sermon on animal blessings. "Beryl, won't you do something?"

"Do something?" she repeated, thinking how wonderful it was Leo had come to her wedding, while the smallest sliver of hope began to grow in her that his owner had come too. *Was Philip somewhere close?*

"Shall I kick it?" Arthur asked. "Perhaps that might make it leave."

"Certainly not!" The idea her fiancé would kick the animal that had saved her life in the alley! Then, caring not a whit if it messed up her satin gown, Beryl bent low and swept Leo off his stout legs, lifting him in her arms. He didn't struggle at all, simply gazing at her soulfully.

"I'm sure he understands the solemnity of the occasion," she said.

"That's absurd," Arthur sputtered.

And then in the silence of the shocked church, Beryl heard a noise overhead. Glancing up at the right-hand balcony, to the second level over the side aisle, she saw *him*.

Looking rather dashing in his black captain's frock coat, with Rufus at his side, Philip Carruthers gave her a small salute. Immediately, Beryl relaxed as the tight knot plaguing her insides all week loosened. Her captain was here, and she was positive it could only mean one thing.

Sure enough, as the entire gathering of guests watched, Philip let down a thick rope which was anchored around one of the elegant Corinthian columns. Quick as a monkey she'd seen at the London Zoo, he climbed down, his booted feet gracefully landing on the tiled nave floor.

One of the female guests screamed, perhaps thinking they were under attack. Then Rufus's laughter echoed in the rafters as he began to haul the rope up. By the time it had died down, Philip had reached the altar.

"Give no quarter, Lord Corsair," called out his first mate.

"What is the meaning of this?" the rector asked.

Beryl stared at Philip Carruthers, realizing she was smiling, feeling relaxed for the first time in a long time.

"I have come to take what's mine," her captain said. Then he spoiled the serious statement by winking at her. Her smile only grew.

"Carruthers, are you insane?" Arthur asked, looking particularly nervous, for Beryl realized Philip had come fully armed with sword and revolver.

"No, Lord Wharton," he replied, not taking his gaze off of her. "I am a pirate!"

The guests began to murmur in earnest. Her father and her cousin approached, and even the groomsmen, though looking reluctant, stepped forward as if to apprehend the intruder.

"Wait," Beryl said, still holding Leo, who seemed as if he might doze off in her arms. "Let him speak. Have you something to say, Captain?"

"I have indeed. Will you come live with me and be my love?"

"I say!" Arthur exclaimed, but Beryl ignored him.

"Though you be a pirate, will you make an honest woman of me?" she asked.

He grinned, and she would have melted at his feet if she hadn't the cat to support.

"I will, sweet lady. If you'll have me. Will you take my name, my heart, my life?"

"Oh, yes," she replied. "I certainly will."

And her captain leaned forward, pulled her to him, squeezing the cat between them, and kissed her.

Pandemonium ensued.

As they broke apart, she saw Arthur blanch, if it were possible for him to become any paler, and then appear to nearly faint into the arms of his groomsmen. Her father's diplomatic voice told everyone to remain calm and seated. Her cousin, the earl, sent a warm smile to his wife, Maggie, Countess of Cambrey, who was seated in the first row, before he shrugged. After all, what could he do?

Glancing toward her mother, hoping she wasn't upset, Beryl received a little nod of approval and then her mother mouthed the words, "I love you!" Her siblings were instantly loud and raucous, and despite her father's words, the youngest two jumped up and began to sing, "Beryl's in love with a pirate!" over and over.

Oh dear!

"If everyone will come back to our home on Cavendish Square," her cousin intoned, "the bridal feast will continue as planned."

Guests who might've feared missing out on the splendor of the Earl of Cambrey's townhouse and his countess's hospitality heaved a general sigh of audible relief, and everyone got to their feet and began to shuffle toward the exit.

Even her parents, after herding her siblings into some semblance of order, left after she gave an encouraging nod of her head.

"I don't suppose we can marry this minute?" Philip asked the rector.

"No, my son. Pirate or no pirate, even you must have a license with the correct names on it."

Arthur had regained his composure and addressed her. "Is this truly what you want?" He gestured at Philip and even encompassed the cat in her arms.

"Yes," she told him. "I'm very sorry, Lord Wharton. I hope you will be extremely happy in your life."

He nodded and turned away. Then he looked back. "May I have the bracelet?"

"Oh!" She really shouldn't be surprised. "Of course." Moreover, she now recalled she would have a lot of presents to return. *What a nuisance!*

She set Leo down at her feet, knowing better than to hand him to Philip. Holding out her wrist to Eleanor, who'd stood silently at her back the entire time, Beryl let her best friend remove the sparkling shackle. Then, she handed it to Arthur. Without another word, he left along with his friends.

She'd been very lucky. He could have made this into an ugly scene, or verbally attacked her, Philip, or her parents.

"He behaved as a true gentleman," she murmured.

"Pish!" Philip said.

"Pish?" she asked, letting him take her hand and thread it under his arm as they began to follow the stragglers out of All Souls.

"He behaved as a man whose heart was barely involved," Philip said. "Elsewise, he would have fought me for you. I certainly would have fought me for you."

She giggled at his foolish turn of phrase. "Which one of you would have won?"

He grinned again. "Undoubtedly, I would have thrashed myself within an inch of my own life to keep you."

Halfway down the nave, he stopped, and her bridesmaids with Eleanor pausing to give her a jaunty, happy wave, continued out of the vestibule's double doors.

Finally, they were alone.

"Now, I can kiss you properly," he told her.

Cradling her face between his hands, he lowered his mouth and claimed her lips in a kiss which made Beryl sizzle down to her toes.

When he drew back, she sighed. "I could not have gone without that the rest of my life."

He nodded. "And there's so much more to experience. Let's start at once, shall we?"

Willingly, she walked by his side, ready to go with him and be ravished.

"Where are you taking me?"

"To our ship, of course!"

Our ship! She liked the sound of that. She would make her home wherever he was.

"Why did you dress that way, as if you were going to sea? And why were you armed?"

Philip laughed. "To show everyone I was a true pirate, of course."

"I always knew you were," she told him.

Beryl glanced back for only one reason, to make sure Leo was following, for he was nearly as dear to her as his owner.

ON BOARD THE *ROBERT*, she soon discovered Mr. Churley had done his duty as a top-notch quartermaster. Even though they dare not show their faces at her bridal breakfast, she and Philip would have plenty of food and wine, and even champagne! They sat down in the galley to break their fast, eating whatever they didn't have to cook—crusty bread and butter, cheese, pickled onions, sliced apples, cold ham, and champagne.

"Not a square of hardtack in sight," Beryl observed gratefully.

"Never when we're within walking distance of a bakery," he confessed.

The only thing missing was the gentle swaying of the hull in the water, but a ship didn't sway in drydock.

Philip assured her that would be rectified soon enough, as her father's stateroom was nearing completion, and then the *Robert* would be launched once again.

Meanwhile, grabbing the open champagne, her captain was eager to take her to his cabin. *Their* cabin, or so it would become when they were married.

Beryl thought his eagerness was for obvious reasons, but when he opened the cabin door and ushered her in, she saw changes that delighted her.

A rug, curtains, a larger wardrobe replaced his old, small one, a second comfortable chair at the table, which itself was larger and sporting a tablecloth. And in the middle of this was the candlestick.

She turned to him.

"You did all this for me?"

He nodded, placing the bottle and his glass on the table, and removing his frock coat, which he rested over the back of a chair.

"I did. I just didn't realize it at first." She watched him lay his sword and his revolver on the table before pulling off his boots. "Not until I showed Rufus yesterday, and he laughed at me for creating a lover's nest without a mate."

"It's perfect," she proclaimed, setting down her own glass.

"It is now you're here."

Before she could react, he swept her up and laid her on the bed, then stretched out beside her.

"A new counterpane," she noticed, stroking her hand across the deep-blue satin.

With a wry smile, he caressed her arm. "Yes, and new sheets and pillows and a towel on the washstand, but if you're going to recite a list of all that's new in here, we'll never get to the best part."

"Which is?" she asked, mystified.

"You. It's been a very long time since you lay in my bed, my love, and the first time I've laid upon it with you."

"That's true. Before, I had only Leo. Where is he, by the way?"

"He is around," Philip promised. "For once, we are not going to think about that blasted cat."

"That perfectly adorable, brave, fearless, courageous, soft cat."

"Those are terms you're supposed to use for me," he protested. "Except for the soft part."

She had to tell him. "I do think all those things about you, except the soft part. I think you're a magnificent man. I have since you rescued me the first time."

"Really?" he asked, his eyebrows drawing together.

"Well, maybe not the very first moment. But you didn't make me use a hole next to the bowsprit, which I still have no idea what that is, and you bought me a clean dress. I was only wary of falling in love—deeply in love—with a pirate."

They stared at one another a long moment.

"I lied," he said, causing her heart to speed up. *Was he married already? In love with a bar wench?*

"What?" she asked, wishing her voice hadn't come out weak and breathy with fear.

"I am utterly soft in one regard. My heart is mush with love for you. Anything you ask of me, I will do if I am capable. I will spend the rest of my days, on sea and on land, loving you."

He paused, ruining the poignant gravity of his words, by adding, "I would like to start the physical aspect immediately."

"We are not married," she pointed out, wanting to hear him state his fervent desire for her, his inability to wait to consummate the love between them.

"We will be," he countered, "as long as you're willing to marry a sea captain."

"The wait is only a fortnight," she reminded him.

"The wait is an eternity," he said, then groaned and rolled onto his back. "You are right, of course. You deserve to be lawfully married before—"

"Before?" she asked, wondering what words he would use for the glorious act.

"Before I make love to you properly."

"*Pish!*" she said.

"*Pish?*" Philip sat up again, leaning on his elbow and looking down at her, merriment dancing in his dark eyes.

"If you *are* a pirate, which I think you are, you had best get started with the plundering, yes?"

Philip threw his head back and laughed. He laughed until tears appeared in the corners of his eyes.

She hoped he wasn't laughing at her, for she very much wanted to be plundered right then. Indeed, she had been thinking of it since first looking up in All Souls and seeing him in his dashing pirate garb.

"Beryl, you are a rare jewel beyond anyone. And it is my privilege to plunder my future bride."

CHAPTER NINETEEN

Taking it slow as treacle poured over sponge cake on a chilly day, Philip removed her satin wedding dress, frilly undergarments, and brand new, extremely tight corset. *Thank God!*

Beryl wanted to rub her sore skin, and even scratch a little, but restrained herself. That wouldn't be very ladylike or enticing.

Instead, she basked in the way he looked at her, the exclamations of endearment as he uncovered more and more of her to his hungry gaze.

Yes, she was going to like passionate love and desire far more than the lukewarm arrangement she'd had with Arthur.

Having Philip undress her was gloriously arousing. However, she was far more interested when he took off his own shirt to reveal a broad chest with flat nipples and a sprinkling of dark hair. *Hm.*

And the ridges of muscle across his stomach drew her hands to his body at once, unable to keep from touching him even as it caused a flutter low in her hips.

She was even more spellbound when he shucked off his pants and—

"Gracious!" she exclaimed, clasping her hand instantly around his stiff shaft as it sprang free. "How on earth did you keep that in there? Why don't men wear larger trousers?"

He didn't seem to be able to speak, kneeling next to her on the bed, his eyes closed as she explored his body.

Finally, his hand whipped out and halted her touch.

"Love, you must stop, or we will be done before we begin."

"I have no idea what you mean. Look." She pointed out the bead of liquid on the end of his manhood.

His laugh sounded pained. Then pushing her down onto the bed, without delay, he covered her mouth with his. Their kiss, as usual, began with a simple melding of mouths, and then his tongue entered her parted lips and began to explore.

She sucked gently on the invading marauder, enjoying the feel of his hands on her skin. And then, as had happened when he'd entered her bedroom weeks earlier, she could feel dampness gathering between her thighs.

"I think I am ready."

Silence.

"Philip?"

He sighed. "Just let me love you. Remember, *I* am the one doing the plundering."

She giggled but stopped as soon as he began to trail kisses down her sensitive skin, drawing her nipples into his hot mouth, one after the other, before going lower to blow on her damp curls.

In fact, by the time he nudged her legs apart and fit the head of his shaft to her opening, she could hardly breathe.

"Hurry," Beryl said, digging her fingers into his buttocks, pulling him toward her.

"It will hurt a little, I'm told," he warned her.

"Oh, then don't hurry. Just—"

He entered her, gliding into the area of her body that was pulsing with need.

"Ow," she uttered.

He froze. "Is it terribly painful?"

"No. You may continue."

Still, he didn't move.

"Really," she assured him, "it doesn't hurt anymore. Carry on ravishing me."

He snickered softly. "This is the strangest—"

"Please, don't tell me you're comparing me to other women whom you've made love to. Or I shall lose all enthusiasm for this undertaking."

"Of course not." Philip dropped a kiss on her lips, a long, unhurried one, even as she could feel his manhood throbbing fiercely inside her.

As he tugged at her lower lip with his teeth, she realized the pulse between her thighs matched the heartbeat in his chest pressed against her own.

What a wondrous thing!

Lifting his head, his dark eyes were glittering with desire, or was that the sheen of love?

"I was only going to say this is the strangest, most polite pirate plundering that ever was. I'm sure of it," he insisted. "And now that I know what it feels like, I promise you I have never *made love* before."

She smiled, tilting her hips in invitation for him to start moving again. Rather urgently now, she wanted the heady, thrilling sensation he'd given her in her bedroom.

He slid farther into her heated channel, and she gasped at the fullness. Then he drew out, and she gasped again as her body seemed to squeeze and hold onto him, causing a delicious tugging feeling.

With easy movements of his hips, Philip repeated the action, gliding in and out, and she wrapped her legs around the back of him, clasping her hands onto his broad shoulders and hanging on.

Panting and lightheaded, the release she sought was just beyond her reach, until he slipped his hand between their bodies and touched the center of her desire, the throbbing nubbin he'd stroked when first he'd touched her in her own bed.

It catapulted her into the heavens, as her coiled pleasure tightened and then expanded with blissful release.

Crying out, she clung to him, feeling his body tense under her touch, and then after a rapid surging motion that filled her completely, he voiced a guttural, exciting sound of absolute masculinity. She felt him spend his warm seed into her womb, and then he settled a moment on top of her, his body heated and his skin damp.

When she was about to beg for air, Philip rolled off of her, and they lay side-by-side staring at the cabin ceiling.

After a moment, she said the first thing that came to her wool-wrapped, exhausted brain. "I'm awfully glad I was kidnapped and you saved me."

Wordlessly, he drew her into his arms, pulled the counterpane over them, and took her with him into a deep, dreamless sleep.

AN INSISTENT SCRATCHING AT the cabin door awakened him, and Philip could see by the waning light through the portholes, they'd slept the day away.

Yesterday, he'd imagined spending this day in the bottom of a bottle of brandy, knowing Beryl was off on her honeymoon. Instead, he'd spent it curled around the woman he loved. *A miracle!*

The clawing sound became more adamant. The moggy was hungry or perhaps thirsty, for Philip might not have remembered to put down a bowl of water. Or, more likely, Leo simply wanted to annoy him.

"You'd best let him in," came her soft voice beside him, "before he ruins the door."

"Why don't you do it," he suggested, "and I'll watch you."

She laughed, a lovely sound. "If he's hungry, he's not the only one. I'm ravenous," she declared.

And just as a pirate's wench should, she got out of bed stark naked and padded across the new rug to the cabin door, letting Philip ogle her backside. He would never get tired of that particular view.

She pulled the door open only a few inches, and Leo strolled in, ran across the rug, and jumped directly onto the tangled bed clothes. Then he froze.

"I think he was hoping you were in the bed, not me," Philip observed.

She poured them each the last of the champagne and sauntered back to him, clearly knowing she had all his attention.

Handing him a glass, she climbed in. Sure enough, the cat relaxed, settling into a warm, round ball *between* them.

Beryl giggled. "I guess he wasn't hungry, but I still am."

"You are insatiable," Philip declared.

"I meant for food," she clarified, sipping the now flat, warm liquid and making a face.

He took the glass from her. "I am and ever will be at your service."

Rising from the bed, he knew she was catching an eyeful of *his* backside, but only for a moment before he slid on his pants.

"Oh," she protested.

"I'm not going on deck without my pants. But I'll be quick. I'm afraid until cook comes onboard, the fare will be more of the same."

"And tea?" she asked.

"If you can wait a minute, I'll light the stove, but I warn you, I'm liable to burn my ship to its rudder. I do have a barrel of fresh water, so we can have tea, and I know I have a pound of sultana cake. How about we eat a little, and then I get you home before your family thinks you've been kidnapped again?"

Glad he could provide the tea she so loved, he hurried out of the cabin. When he returned, she was dressed, though he noticed she'd left a few layers on the cabin floor.

Setting the cake and tea upon the table, he pulled out her chair.

As if they were both beacons of civilized society, she nodded her gratitude, took the seat, and let him push her in. He paused only to don his shirt.

They ate and drank in comfortable silence for a moment, and he fervently hoped she had no regrets.

"In case you are wondering, I will go to a magistrate today and get a license."

She nodded her agreement, chewing thoughtfully.

"And I will go to your father," he added, "and make my formal request for his blessing."

She shrugged. "It seems a little late for that, but it would be respectful."

"And will you be happy to come on voyages with me?"

Her eyes got a little rounder. "As long as we're not going to the Orient."

"Never again," Philip promised. "Not even if Queen Victoria herself asks me."

That engendered her bright smile.

"It's all so very different from the life I'd expected," she mused, and her words sliced at his happiness.

"I'm sorry." The words tumbled out of his mouth, even as his heart plummeted, for she seemed to be expressing regret.

"No, don't be. You misunderstand me." She set down her mug of tea with a thump. "I cannot tell you how glad I am not to have to do what was planned for me. The feeling of suffocation which caused me to go with my father on his long voyage has entirely lifted."

He stared at her, her hair completely loose around her shoulders, her wrinkled gown, her sparkling eyes, drinking tea, eating cake—looking well-tupped.

"I cannot promise you will have anything like a viscountess's life," he told her, "but I can promise it will be an adventure."

"I would expect nothing less from Lord Corsair."

He felt the familiar heat of embarrassment.

"Now, will you tell me why your men call you that?"

Philip couldn't help rolling his eyes. "I made the mistake of telling Rufus about a game my brother and I played as children in Newquay. Of course, we were always pretending to be pirates, building boats out of whatever wood we had and begging fabric off our mother for sails. We wanted to be bloodthirsty and bold, like the Barbary corsairs. It seemed for a century or more, they controlled the seas. And we learned every story we could, and found them all fascinating."

In fact, he only then recalled a particular one. "I just remembered an English corsair named Henry Mainwaring was even knighted in the seventeenth century."

"Just like you," she interrupted.

He laughed. "Now there was a captain with a good moniker, *The Dread Pirate*."

She tilted her head and considered him. "It wouldn't suit you." She popped another morsel of buttery sultana cake into her mouth. "You are more dash-fire than dread. Please continue."

"More dash-fire than dread?" he echoed, reaching over to wipe a crumb from her lips. "Anyway, my father became a baronet by appointment from the queen, and Rufus delights in making fun, in conjuring a mincing dandy trying to be a brutal corsair."

"But you are *not* a mincing dandy. I know. I've met a few."

Philip didn't want to think for a moment of the men she'd known before him, even if only on a ballroom dance floor. Grasping her arm, he tugged her until she stood, and then he hauled her onto his lap.

"Then what am I?"

She took his face in her hands, and he knew he could stare into her fawn-like eyes forever.

"Oh, that's simple," she said. "You're a pirate, of course."

And she leaned down, claimed his lips, and plundered his mouth as only Lady Corsair could do.

EPILOGUE

One Year Later

"Be careful," Beryl yelled, hoping the wind didn't whip her words away to the other side of the cove.

Then she shook her head. *Pointless!*

Two of her younger brothers were splashing in the water with Philip, who'd fashioned a sailboat for them to take turns learning how to "haul wind," as her skilled husband put it. He'd already taught them all how to swim during an earlier visit, including her two sisters who sat at the water's edge with her youngest brother.

Her parents were somewhere on the other side of the peninsula having a quiet day, which Beryl didn't begrudge them one whit.

Philip came bounding up the beach toward where she was setting up a picnic around Leo, sunning himself on one end of the table her husband and brothers had dragged onto the sand.

"What on God's blue-watered earth do we need to be careful of, woman?" he asked, merriment in his beloved dark eyes.

She shrugged. "I don't want them to go out too far in case . . ."

He put his hands on his hips. "In case there are pirates in the cove?"

She offered him a smile.

"There's already one right here on the beach," she teased but sent a glance past him to her siblings.

Philip took the pitcher of lemonade out of her hand, set it beside the cat, who opened his eyes, hissed, then stretched lazily amongst the stack of plates, though she'd put the basket of bread and the cold meats at the other end. Leo closed his eyes again.

"That's rather disgusting," her husband remarked. "There'll be fur in the food."

Then he took her in his arms.

"Come now, Lady Carruthers," for so she was called as a knight's wife, which he never tired of saying. "You are usually so fearless. What has got into you?"

"Everything is simply so perfect," she confessed. "I want it to stay this way. My family is so happy. Thank you." She pressed her cheek against his chest.

This wasn't the Angsleys first trip to her and Philip's Newquay home. For this two-week visit to the Cornish coast, her family had arrived by train a week earlier. Her parents had rented a cottage close by, though her brothers and sisters spent most of the time at her house, and only went back to their rented home to sleep.

And, in any case, they spent nearly all day, every day on the beach, and when they weren't, they were exploring the caves or flying kites.

Philip had talked of adding on to his boyhood home when he'd first brought her to Cornwall. Between her family and his, they seemed to always have visitors who wanted to enjoy a seaside holiday.

Beryl had protested. For when they were not living on the *Robert*, taking her father back and forth to Spain, their coastal home seemed positively palatial. She hadn't imagined it would need to be larger.

However, she now knew things were soon to change. She had no idea why she'd kept the glorious secret to herself. Perhaps it was the bustle of cleaning and preparing for her family's visit. Or maybe it was simply that saying something out loud would make it real, and then their lives would irrevocably alter.

Suddenly, though, she couldn't keep it to herself any longer.

"I missed my monthly flow," she muttered against her husband's warm body.

She felt Philip grow entirely still. Then his arms tightened, even as he drew back and looked down at her.

"What did you say?"

"My courses have stopped." There, she'd finally said it plainly.

He paused, a myriad of emotions fluttering across his handsome, tanned face.

"Do you mean you're carrying our child?"

"That's usually what it means." She offered him a tentative smile. "*Promptus et fidelis,*" she added, which had become her mantra since marrying this wonderful man.

"Well, sink me!" he exclaimed.

Throwing his head back as if he were bellowing up to the crow's nest, he yelled, "A child. My child!" Then he looked down at her again and grinned, sending her insides into a spiral of longing and love.

"*Our* child," he whispered. "The luckiest on earth."

In the next instant, he swept her off her feet, cradling her high against his chest. Beryl always felt safe held in his strong arms and often stroked their sculpted muscles when lying beside him during the peaceful, salty nights at sea or at home—arms meant for building boats and raising sails and for levering his tantalizing body over hers in bed when he made love to her and for . . .

Carrying her to the water?

"Our child will love the ocean as I do," her joyful captain said.

"Philip!" she cried out as he strode with her straight into the gentle sea.

The cool water contrasted with the warm sun, making her cling to him and shiver.

"You are mad!"

She heard her siblings laughing and then the teasing response of her husband.

"No, my lady. I'm a pirate!"

Finis

ABOUT THE AUTHOR

USA Today bestselling author Sydney Jane Baily writes historical romance set in Victorian England, late 19th-century America, the Middle Ages, the Georgian era, and the Regency period. She believes in happily-ever-after stories for an already-challenging world with engaging characters and attention to period detail.

Born and raised in California, she has traveled the world, spending a lot of exceedingly happy time in the U.K. where her extended family resides, eating fish and chips, drinking shandy, and snacking on Maltesers and Cadbury bars. Sydney currently lives in New England with her family—human, canine, and feline.

You can learn more about her books and contact her via her website at SydneyJaneBaily.com.